He tilted his head, confused.

"But you don't hang out with anyone else?"

Fiona shook her head. "I have lived here for a few years, but haven't put in much effort to make friends. So it's my own fault."

He pushed himself off the rock he was leaning against and crossed to her. He reached out a hand, pulling her up straight too. Hannah babbled cheerfully between them as Sam smiled down at them, shaking Fiona's hand. "Well, allow me to introduce myself. I'm Sam Tiernan, officially your friend."

He had no idea how isolating her job had been. His work friends were more like his family and he had lived here his entire life. Sam knew just about everyone in this town, but he had more than enough room for one more friend in his life. Especially one as kind and giving as Fiona.

Her eyes sparkled as she shook his hand back. "Nice to meet you, friend."

He was reluctant to let her hand go.

Julie Brookman is a former preacher's kid who started her career after college as the manager of a bookstore, later becoming a journalist and public relations specialist. She has spent her whole life with her nose in a book and loves stories with happily-ever-afters. Besides writing sweet and inspirational romance novels, Julie enjoys hiking, reading and belting out show tunes at the top of her lungs (which leads to strange looks from other drivers she passes). Julie lives in Michigan with her husband, her three awesome kids and her kitty, Pepper Potts. Visit her website at www.authorjuliebrookman.com.

Books by Julie Brookman

Love Inspired

His Temporary Family

Visit the Author Profile page at LoveInspired.com for more titles.

His Temporary Family

Julie Brookman

LOVE INSPIRED
INSPIRATIONAL ROMANCE

LOVE INSPIRED®
INSPIRATIONAL ROMANCE

Recycling programs for this product may not exist in your area.

ISBN-13: 978-1-335-58565-3

His Temporary Family

Love Inspired
22 Adelaide St. West, 41st Floor
Toronto, Ontario M5H 4E3, Canada
www.LoveInspired.com

Printed in U.S.A.

As we have therefore opportunity,
let us do good unto all men, especially
unto them who are of the household of faith.
—*Galatians* 6:10

For my Valley of the Sun writing friends.
Thank you for your support and encouragement,
it has meant the world to me. Not to mention
all the online write-ins to help me focus and get
words on the page. This book would not exist
without you. Keep on writing, ladies.
The world needs your stories.

Chapter One

Fiona Shay walked in the door of her ancient Victorian house and kicked off her heels right next to the entrance. Her feet were aching all day, but she loved how the shoes made her feel taller and more put together. In social work, anything that gave you strength and confidence was a good thing.

"Honey, I'm home," she called, and her dog Sherlock lifted his head to give her an unimpressed look before returning to his nap. Fiona chuckled.

"I love you, too, buddy."

Her first stop was the kitchen, where she checked on her dinner. Fiona cringed at the smell that was coming out of the slow cooker.

"I don't think this one is a winner," she said out loud. It was so confusing. She had followed the recipe to the letter but somehow managed to mess it up. Fiona was tempted to take a taste of it, but she resisted. That was for later, because she had promised the person helping her learn to cook that they would try everything together.

Just because Fiona had to wait to eat, didn't mean everyone in the house had to. She filled Sherlock's food and water bowls. This finally drew his interest, causing him to rush to his feet and toward the kitchen. She gave him a scratch behind his ears. "It's okay. Sometimes I don't move unless someone's offering food, either."

Fiona cleaned up from her day quickly, knowing that her old hot water heater wouldn't last long. The pipes were still creaking once the water was off, another sign of the age of her house. Fiona would need to have someone look at the plumbing. She inherited this house from her nana a few years ago, and with it a laundry list of repairs she would need to make.

Fiona moved to Basswood Corners five years ago when her grandmother had gotten sick, and she didn't have the heart to sell the home after her death and leave because it was the only thing she had left of her favorite person. Nor did she have the heart to make many changes to the place her grandmother so lovingly decorated, despite her mother's constant insistence that it was time to make it her own.

But she had looked up to Nana and loved everything about her. Fiona grew up wanting to be just like her, so it made sense to live in this house without changes, even if it felt like it was falling down around her sometimes.

She dressed in a cozy pair of yoga pants and a hoodie, running her fingers through her hair to get all the knots out before heading into the kitchen. Her wild curls could not be tamed, but she didn't mind. She had something more exciting to do. With a smile, she pulled an envelope out of her purse.

"It was a busy day, Nana, but we saved a few more,"

Fiona announced as she entered the end where her grandmother used to sit and relax at the end of her day. She wasn't there anymore, but Fiona kept with her daily tradition now that she had followed in her career footsteps and became a caseworker. First, she wrote in the journal next to the chair.

"Three kids now have a safe roof over their heads and food in their stomachs."

Pulling a paper that was scribbled on in all kinds of crayon and signed with sloppy letters on the bottom, Fiona smiled. This one, drawn by a little girl who was waiting in her office while she found her an emergency placement with a foster family, would be added to the box of other art projects so lovingly made by kids in care. She kept every one, just like her grandmother had.

Finally, she pulled out a picture of one of her former clients at the courthouse with her new parents after their adoption was finalized. A found family and a safe childhood.

That was the goal…along with filling up as many keepsake boxes of the happy part of social work as her Nana had. Though she saw some terrible things on the job, looking at all these happy things was a great reminder that it was all worth it. Maybe someday she would surpass her nana's legend around town for helping people and be a real credit to the woman's legacy.

But first, she had to go fail at dinner. Again.

Sherlock's bowl was almost empty by the time Fiona reentered the kitchen. "Will you be okay while I bring Carol her food, buddy?"

Her dog just continued to devour his food, but Fiona

nodded as if he had replied. "Yeah, thanks, I'll miss you, too. I'll be back soon."

Fiona poured some of her attempt at tortilla soup into a food storage container, and packed the tortilla chips, cheese and avocado slices that went with it into another. Her next-door neighbor, Carol, was trying to teach her slow cooker recipes after noticing how much Fiona relied on takeout and microwave dinners after a long day of work.

The only problem was—Fiona had never learned her way around the kitchen and seemed to mess up everything she tried to make. Still, Carol was patient and encouraged her to keep trying. And she made Fiona promise not to try any of the food until they were together. "I'll be honest with you, and we both know you're too hard on yourself," she said.

Carol had been her grandmother's best friend, and she had kind of adopted Fiona as her own grandchild after Nana passed. They saw each other almost every day, except on Sundays when her family came to spend time with her and run errands. Fiona never wanted to intrude.

Her cell phone rang as she was on her way out the door. "Mom, can I call you back? I'm just heading out."

There was the telltale throat clearing on the other end of the line that told Fiona that she was in for another lecture from her mother. She wondered what it would be this time. She needed to sell Nana's house and move back to the city to be near them? That she was wasting her life as a social worker? That it was time for her to settle down and get married?

"All right, if you don't have time to talk to your mother,

I will be quick about it, then," Violet Shay's Southern drawl responded. "I'm just calling to tell you that your father and I are remodeling the house for a few months and won't have a guest room available for you if you decide to honor us with a visit."

And there it was, the subtle reminder that she hadn't been home in a long time.

"That's fine. I don't think I'll be able to get away from the office in the next few months anyway. Maybe you and Daddy can come out here for a visit once things settle down for you."

Fiona almost giggled at her own words. Her parents, who lived in the wealthy suburbs of Charleston, hated the small town in Colorado where she had settled. Her mother had grown up here but wanted to leave it in the past.

"Instead, you could take some time off to come visit your parents and see all your friends here," her mother said. "They work you too hard there."

Fiona sighed. "They have to. There are so many kids in need."

"I love the big heart you have, but you can't save the whole world, Fiona. And it's high time you accepted that and start living your own your life."

Fiona squeezed her eyes shut in frustration. Her mother didn't fully understand the desire to work in the trenches as Fiona did, helping struggling families thrive and children grow up safe and happy.

"I *am* living my life, Mama. The life I want to live."

Well, mostly. She barely had any time to do anything outside work, but she loved her job. She would have time for fun later.

Her mother sighed at the other end of the line. "But you're all alone."

And there it was…the reminder of her obligation to get married and have lots of grandchildren. "I'm not alone. I have Sherlock."

There was a scoff on the other end of the line. "While my grand-dog is very cute, he doesn't count. I just want to see you settled down and happy."

Now was probably not the time to tell her mother all the terrible things she saw on the job as a result of people falling in love and getting married. She would rather be alone than go through what some of these couples did. "I have to go, Mama. I'll try to schedule some time off to visit when you're done with the house. I hope your renovation goes well."

There was a deep sigh, but then her mother finally gave up on the conversation and said her goodbyes.

Fiona eyed the soup on the counter, wondering if it would be more appetizing now that it was lukewarm instead of piping hot. "It can't be any worse, I'm guessing," she told Sherlock, who promptly rolled over for a belly rub.

She obliged before heading to the door. Fiona put a hat over her wet hair to keep it from getting too cold, then crossed from her driveway to the next. A little path had formed between the bushes that divided the driveways, thanks to the number of times Fiona went this way.

She knocked on the front door. "Carol, it's Fiona! Are you there?"

Carol came to the door in her pajamas, and Fiona envied her ability to get cozy so early in the evening.

She had told Fiona once that she sometimes just wore her pajamas all day if she had nowhere to go.

Life goals, Fiona thought. She loved her work, but her mother might be right about her needing some serious downtime to prevent burnout. She had seen it happen far too often with her colleagues. But there was always so much to do.

Carol's hair was more out of place than usual, and her normal welcoming smile was missing.

"Oh, Fiona, I completely forgot you were coming. This day has gotten so far away from me. So much has been going on."

Fiona arched a brow at her friend's words. She noticed that Carol's shoulders were slumped, and her eyes were tight with worry. She reached out and squeezed her friend's hand.

"You know I'm always going to be here with dinner, rain or shine, busy or not. I wouldn't miss stopping by for the world. I need to see my second favorite cat."

As if on cue, Carol's Russian Blue breed cat, Sylvia, with smooth gray fur and bright yellow eyes, purred and rubbed against Fiona's leg. "Hey, sweet girl. You're really trying to make my dog jealous now."

Sherlock, a senior mutt she adopted from the shelter last year, was not a fan of the cat smell that came home with Fiona from her visits with Carol. Before she reached down and gave the cat a pet, she handed the bowl of soup to the older woman. She looked at it with relief.

"Oh, dinner would actually be very welcome right now. I didn't know what we were going to eat," Carol said. Fiona looked up at her with worry again. Nana started getting dementia in her later years, losing her train of thought here and there. She wondered if the same thing was happening to her friend.

"Are you doing okay? I can just put the dinner in the fridge and let you rest for a bit if you'd like."

Carol shook her head, as if clearing her thoughts. "No, I'm fine, dear. It's just been a really hard day for my family."

Before Fiona could ask anything further, a man appeared behind Carol. She jumped at the newcomer, and it took her a few moments to realize that it was Carol's grandson, whom she had seen over at the house from time to time. And she couldn't put her finger on it, but Fiona thought maybe she had seen him somewhere else before as well.

The man looked a little worse for wear now, however. His hair was a wild mess, sticking out in every direction.

He had a panicked look in his eyes that had Fiona looking around to make sure there wasn't a fire or some other catastrophe in Carol's house.

"Oh, good, you two can finally meet," Carol said with a smile as she winked at Fiona. Her stress from earlier seemed to be gone now. "This is my grandson, Sam. He's the one that I've been telling you about."

Fiona almost backed out the door and ran away, because Carol had been hinting about her dating her grandson for about a year now. But before she could even move, the man grabbed her wrist—albeit gently— and pulled her farther into the house.

"Is that food? Good, I can finally feed them."

Sam pulled the containers of soup out of her hand

before she could object and carried them to the kitchen. "You probably don't want to eat that," she warned, not wanting him to take a bite of her failure at soup.

She followed him into the kitchen and stopped in shock at what she saw there. A baby was in a high chair next to the table and a toddler was sitting in a booster seat, crying.

Fiona didn't know what situation she just walked into, but her soup would probably make everything even worse.

Sam dug around Gran's cupboards, looking for bowls that were made of plastic so the girls couldn't break them. He had no idea what he was doing when it came to taking care of his nieces, but he at least had considered that glassware and little ones did not mix. Gran was a traditionalist, though, and most of her dishes were very breakable. He settled on two ancient Tupperware containers to put their soup in.

"You really don't want to give them that. It might not be edible," his rescuer said from the entryway of the kitchen.

He ignored her words. As long as it was food and maybe stopped Hannah from crying, it would do. She had not stopped since he picked them up from the babysitter a few hours ago after his parents called to say that his brother and sister-in-law had been in a terrible car accident. He had wanted to rush to the hospital, but his family needed him to take care of his nieces. So that was what he would do.

Sam dished up food for the girls, making sure to only give a few little bite-size pieces for 13-month-old Hannah along with some smashed up avocado. Bethany, his sister-in-law, let him give her French fries last time they were together, as long as he gave them to her in tiny pieces. Thankfully, he didn't have to stock up on baby food immediately. He loaded up Hazel's plate as well, hoping it would make the preschooler happy. Sam knew that chicken nuggets were her usual go-to food, but this would have to do.

Little smiles appeared on their faces, and he felt better right away. When he first arrived at their house, they were thrilled to see him, but after a while, the toddler had started asking where mommy and daddy were, and things had gone downhill from there. He brought them over to Gran's, hoping that she would be able to help cheer them up, but she was worried, too.

This had been a long day for everyone. And things would probably not go back to normal for a long time—maybe ever.

Hopefully, this food would help, even if just a little bit.

"Thank you so much. I was wondering if I was going to have to make a hamburger run or something. Have a seat and I'll get some for you and Gran," Sam said.

The woman, whom he assumed was the neighbor Gran was always going on about, sat down nervously at the table. "I was being serious. That soup is not going to be very good."

Gran sat down next to her and patted her hand. "Nonsense. Remember, I told you that you have to let others be the judge because you're too hard on yourself."

Sam put the bowls in front of them and sat down himself. Gran said grace, mentioning his brother Benjamin, his sister-in-law and his parents. Sam hadn't heard from them since their first phone call to him this afternoon so there must not be any news yet.

"If you don't mind my asking, why the impromptu family dinner and the frazzled expressions when you came to the door? Is there anything going on that I can help with?"

Sam finally took a moment to study the woman before him. Her blond hair fell in curly waves around her head, and she wore clothing that seemed more like she was ready to head to bed, not to someone's house. Still, her kind eyes exuded comfort. He felt the urge to pour out his soul to her—no wonder she was a social worker. Luckily, his grandmother explained so he wouldn't have to.

Gran filled her in on Benjamin's accident, quietly so as not to draw the girls' attention. "Both of them are in critical condition. All we can do is hope and pray."

Sad eyes turned to him. "This must be hard for you to not be there at the hospital with your brother."

Sam's jaw clenched as he looked out the window. "Yeah, but I'm needed here. I don't know how to take care of babies, but I'll do what I can so my parents can be there for them."

"I'm so sorry. Let me know if there is anything I can do," Fiona said, her eyes filling with tears.

He raised his spoon. "You've helped out enough by bringing us dinner."

She cringed at that. Sam looked nervously at Gran. It couldn't taste that bad, could it?

He took a bite. It was that bad. He drank down his glass of water in one gulp and then rushed to the fridge for some milk to get the taste of overwhelming spice and burnt chicken out of his mouth. Gran and her neighbor also were sputtering and spitting out their soup.

"I'm so sorry, but that was the worst soup I've ever tasted," he said.

The entire table burst out into laughter.

"Well, I guess I'll have to try again sometime and figure out what I missed in the recipe," she said with a frown.

Sam's brow furrowed. He recognized that frown, and suddenly he remembered exactly where he had seen Gran's neighbor before. He had only seen her a few times, but her stern expression was unforgettable. "Miss Shay?"

She looked at him quizzically. "Do I know you? Other than from here?"

Sam nodded. "Don't you come to the fire station to give the talk on the safe havens every year?"

Fiona smiled in recognition. "I thought you looked familiar. Are you a firefighter?"

Gran gave his shoulder a loving squeeze. "Yes, and the best one they've got."

Sam rolled his eyes at her words, but he felt his cheeks warm a bit at the compliment. Gran looked between them, confused. "What's a safe haven?"

Fiona explained how the fire station was one of the few places a parent could leave a baby they were unwilling or unable to care for, no questions asked. "It eliminates the possibility of them being left on someone's doorstep, exposed to the elements, while waiting for someone to answer a doorbell ring like they did in the old days."

Gran grimaced at that. "I've heard about that happening a few times. But why did you have to talk to the firefighters? Don't they just turn the baby over to you?"

Fiona shook her head. "Small children and infants form strong attachments in their young lives, and whenever those attachments are removed, it can cause lasting damage. So when they are with the firefighters, they are already experiencing a trauma from their separation from their mother that may be with them forever. We train the firefighters to do what they can to mitigate that trauma."

Sam's eyes caught on his two nieces, who were ignoring the adults and in their own little world together. How he helped them over the next couple of days would make a big difference in how they handled this nightmare. It was a lot of responsibility. He prayed that he could handle it.

Fiona must have read the worries on his face because she turned her calming smile on him. "They are so blessed to have you here for them."

Sam gave her a grateful smile for the encouragement. She looked so different from the stern woman he met at the fire station. Her blond hair was wild and curly around her head and not in its normal bun. She was wearing yoga pants and a hoodie, and were those tennis shoes on her feet? Sam had thought she didn't own anything other than heels. She seemed like a completely different person. "Thank you, Miss Shay."

"You can call me Fiona. It only seems fair since you were almost poisoned by my soup," she said, her eyes sparkling with laughter.

Sam tried to reconcile the Miss Shay he remembered

from the station with the Fiona in front of him. How was it that the strict social worker and the sweet woman his grandma always talked about were the same person?

"The soup wasn't that bad, dear. I think you just added too much taco seasoning. I'll order us a pizza," Gran said.

Fiona arched a brow. "Why didn't you do that before I got here?"

Sam kind of wished they had, but there had been no time. "I think we were still in shock. The girls had a snack at their babysitters, and we were just starting to figure out what we were going to do when you showed up at the door, with food already in hand. In retrospect, we should have probably not counted on that to feed us."

He took a big drink of milk to get the soup's taste out of his mouth again.

Gran was smiling as she looked between the two of them. "I'm so glad the two of you have already met. And here I was thinking of ways to try to get my favorite people in the same room."

Fiona's cheeks pinkened a little. "Well, it would have been an easier job than I had down at the fire station. It was kind of hard to pin all of those firefighters down into one room for long enough to do the training. I had to reschedule it three times before we finally were able to complete it."

Sam gave an apologetic shrug. "Our shifts are chaotic. Sometimes we will go for hours with no call at all, and then other days it seems like we have barely enough time to breathe, let alone eat or sleep."

Today had been one of those days. They had gotten two calls at once—he had reported to a fire in an apartment building that they were able to put out quickly. The other engine had been sent to the car accident involving his brother. He would never forget the grim yet supportive expressions on the faces of his peers as his captain gave him the news.

Fiona cast a concerned glance toward Hazel and Hannah. She sighed. "It's fine. We got it done eventually. Sometimes you have to adjust your plans because of unexpected events," she said to Sam, indicating she understood all too well the turmoil their family was in right now. She probably saw situations like this on the job.

Sam fought a yawn, suddenly exhausted. This morning seemed like so long ago, and she was right. His entire world had changed since then.

Gran gave him a concerned look. "You okay, Sammie?"

Suddenly, it all seemed so overwhelming. Should he take the kids to their home so they could sleep in their own beds? Or should he bring them to his apartment and set up the portable crib for the baby? Did he have enough diapers? Food?

Then there was the issue of what was happening— how much did he share with them? Hazel was old enough that she would figure out something was wrong, but he didn't feel qualified to tell her. Sam ran into dangerous situations every day for his job, but facing this new challenge made him want to flee in the other direction. "I don't think I can do this."

Fiona gave him an encouraging smile. "I think that you can. You need to have more faith in yourself. I see people go through emergency foster placements of their nieces, nephews and grandchildren all the time, and they step up and do what needs to be done. You've got this."

Gran sat up in her chair. "That's a great idea!"

Sam and Fiona looked at her, confused. Gran continued, pointing a finger between Fiona and Sam.

"Oh, this is perfect."

Sam was a little nervous at the gleeful look in Gran's eye. He tilted his head at his grandmother. "What?"

She leaned forward and grabbed Fiona's hand. "You can help Sam over the next few days because you've done this kind of thing before. You help families in crisis. You are just what he needs."

Sam couldn't help but notice the grimace on Fiona's face. She had offered to be of help to the family earlier, but perhaps she suspected, as he did, that this was part of Carol's matchmaking scheme for the two of them.

Sam sighed and leaned back in his chair. "Gran, Fiona has her own life and job and can't spend all her time bailing me out."

Although he protested the agreement, Sam couldn't help the hopeful feeling that bubbled at the idea of assistance with the girls.

Gran huffed. "It's Friday, so she has the next few days off. She won't be missing work at all."

Fiona snorted at Gran's volunteering her, but with four pairs of pleading eyes—even the baby's—looking in her direction, she had no defense. "All right, I will help you get set up so you can manage without feeling like the sky is going to fall at any moment."

For the first time today, Sam felt his mood lift. He

wasn't in this alone. "You have no idea how much this means to me. What do we start with?"

Fiona gave him a small smile. "I think we're going to have to go with baby cleanup."

His brow furrowed. "Why?"

She pointed at the high chair, and he followed her gaze. Sam groaned when he saw that Hannah was covered from head to toe with not only her soup, but somehow Hazel's as well.

"I think they realized my cooking was better as a decoration than a meal."

He made an attempt to wipe some of the soup off Hannah, but only smeared it more. The baby had the audacity to giggle at him.

"Do you need my help with this?" Fiona asked.

The baby grinned up at him as if she was proud of her mess. "Nah, I think I can handle this bit." He was a novice, but how hard could it really be to clean up one little baby?

Chapter Two

God put babies and toddlers on earth to test everyone's patience, Sam thought as he wiped smears of chunky soup off Hannah in the bathroom sink. Fiona's company was pleasant, but now he had another reason to never want to be near the recipe she attempted tonight ever again.

"Why did you do this, baby girl? I know the soup was bad, but that doesn't mean we dump it all over ourselves. You could have just pushed it aside."

Hannah just clapped her baby hands on his cheeks, and he leaned forward and kissed her. He was a confirmed bachelor, but he sure did love his nieces. In fact, he excelled at the "fun uncle" role. But when it came to their care and keeping, he was useless.

Sam had tried it once to help his brother out when he was over at their house watching a football game. It was nearly impossible to do anything for her, because Hannah liked to crawl away from him every time he turned away from her. Benjamin had just laughed at him, called him helpless and took over the job.

But he wouldn't have his big brother bailing him out this time—he had to do this on Benjamin's behalf now.

It would be worse this time because judging from the smell, her crawling over the comforter in Gran's guest room would create quite a mess.

"Okay, baby girl. We're in this together. We can do this. You just have to work with me here," Sam said. Hannah just gave a baby squeal of delight and crawled around on the floor. Thankfully, he had already cleaned her hands, but Sam winced when he saw that he had forgotten her knees and smears of soup got onto the carpet. "This is going well already," he murmured.

He sighed and dug through the diaper bag and was relieved to find some extra clothes, wipes and diapers. He would restock soon, but first he needed to focus on the task at hand.

He just about had her all finished when Hannah made her stealth ninja move. He turned to grab more wipes and then she was gone, giggling and crawling away. "We were almost there, you little escape artist. This was supposed to be a team effort."

Hazel was laughing by his side, too, having come into the room to watch him fail miserably. He couldn't be annoyed with Hannah, not when her antics had them both smiling. They deserved every moment of joy they could find right now. If he could fill up their emotional cups with happiness, maybe the hard days ahead would be a little more bearable.

"We have a runner…or a crawler, I guess," Fiona said from the door as she picked Hannah up and carried the squiggling baby back to Sam.

"Yeah, she does that. I'm going to have to figure out how to get her to stop."

Fiona grinned. She tickled Hannah's belly while Sam finished wiping soup from between her toes, wondering how it got in there.

"I think you're going to have to get used to grabbing things one-handed. And if you have to turn your head, put a hand on her belly right here, so you will be able to feel if she's going to make a break for it," Fiona said.

She grabbed Sam's hand and placed it on Hannah's stomach. He shook his head in amazement. "I can't believe I didn't think of that. Thanks. You know a lot about babies. Do you have kids of your own?"

Fiona shook her head and shrugged. "Nope. I've just been a caseworker for a long time. I've been around a lot of kids."

Sam thought that must be a tough job, to meet kids when they are going through something terrible. It took a special person to take that on, and from what he could tell, Fiona was perfect for it.

"Well, I will take any and all advice from you, my friends, strangers passing me on the street," he joked.

Her eyes filled with amusement. "Well, my first suggestion is that you retry the whole onesie thing. You somehow managed to put it on upside down and sideways. I didn't even know that was possible."

Sam groaned as he studied his baby niece. Her outfit did look like it fit a little funny, but he never could understand how those things worked.

"I can't even get the basics right," he murmured.

Fiona tilted her head and stared at him from the side for a moment. "I think you should make a list of any questions you have and then reach out to the people you know. This community is full of people who are parents that can help you."

Sam thought of some of the men on his crew who were parents, and about the ones who scoffed at the idea of settling down with a family. "I usually get along with the bachelor types, since we have more in common. I guess I finally have something to talk to the others about. They probably would love to chat about their kids."

He hated the idea of people knowing just how terrible he was at handling all this. "I probably won't hear the end of it when they learn about my temporary lot in life. They love to tease me about how I have it easy because I don't have any kids."

Fiona's lips turned up as she stood. Some of her blond hair fell out of the ponytail she had put it in during dinner, and one curl came to rest on her cheek. "It's okay to need help. I know your grandmother kind of 'volun-told' me to help you, but seriously, if there is anything I can do to help…just let me know. Your grandmother has my number."

After his attempt to try something with the baby all on his own had been a disaster, he would definitely be taking her up on that. "You should be expecting several frantic phone calls."

Fiona just nodded as he gathered up the girls' things so they could leave. Hazel was excited to help load up the baby's bag. "What's your name? I'm Hazel," the little girl said, pointing to herself.

"My name is Fiona, but you can call me Fi if that's easier," she said.

The little girl gave her a slobbery grin. "Fi! Fi!"

"FiFiFiFiFi," Hannah babbled.

"They like you already," Sam said, throwing the diaper bag over the shoulder of the arm not carrying Hannah.

"Hey, Hazel, how about some pizza with Gran before we head to the store to get supplies?"

There were probably supplies at their house, but going into that home while his brother was fighting for his life seemed like an unbearable prospect at the moment. He would tackle that tomorrow.

The little girl shouted with glee before running out of the room to Gran. Fiona laughed. "See, you're a natural already."

Not at parenting. Pizza he could do. Other things, not so much. "I'm a natural at the fun uncle thing."

The doorbell rang and Fiona went to help Gran with the pizza, but before she turned to leave, she put her hand on his arm. "They need their fun uncle, too. Sure, they need you to take care of them, but based on my experience, I can tell you that young children form very intense attachments and the loss of those attachments can do a lot of damage. The girls may not know everything that is going on, but they will start missing their parents soon. Having someone they are close to around will help. They need you to be *you* right now. Their fun uncle that loves them and always makes sure that they have something to be happy about."

Sam hadn't even thought about that. He had been so worried about figuring out how to make sure the girls were cared for in the physical sense, that he hadn't put a lot of thought into what he could do to cheer them up.

He had a lot of thinking to do, but in the meantime, he put the girls back in their seats for dinner, take two. He also removed all evidence of the toxic soup.

"That soup was yucky. Don't tell Fi," Hazel said, scrunching up her nose.

Sam laughed. "Fi already knows, but she's going to try to make it better next time."

Hazel gave him a horrified look. "No more. It's yucky."

"I heard that," Fiona said as she brought in the pizza and set it on the counter. "I'll make you eat two bowls."

She tickled Hazel, who started giggling hysterically. "No, Fi! I will has one bite! That's it."

Fiona kissed the girl on the forehead, then turned to grab her a slice of pizza, cutting it up into smaller bite-size pieces. Sam couldn't wipe the smile off his face at the scene. She was so good with kids. He wished it were as easy for him. He was hesitant to give the baby more food because she had eaten a little already and he didn't want another mess. Fiona saved the day by digging out some Goldfish and Cheerios she found in Hannah's diaper bag, along with some tiny pieces of sliced banana.

Soon, he would be heading home with the girls to his apartment—he would be solely responsible for their care. Could he even handle it? He loved the bachelor life and had no immediate plans to settle down. Sam enjoyed the freedom to go where he wanted, when he wanted. And while he was going to support his family while they were in need, he couldn't help but feel the shackles already tightening around his freedom.

"You okay over there, Sammie? You just turned white," Gran said, ruffling the hair off his forehead.

He didn't know if it was sheer exhaustion from his long day, his worry for his brother, or being handed this responsibility, but Sam suddenly wanted to crawl into bed and never come out.

As Hazel and Hannah engaged each other in some very serious baby talk, Sam whispered to Gran and Fiona, "Yeah…just…everything just caught up with me again. It's been an incredibly long day."

The two women exchanged a look, making him feel uneasy. He was missing something. "What is it?"

Sam could feel Fiona's sympathetic gaze covering him as Gran reached for his hand and whispered, "Sammie, I just got a call from the hospital. Bethany didn't make it."

He choked back the sob that threatened to erupt. His sister-in-law, who had started dating his brother when they were only teenagers, was no longer in this world.

Sam's eyes rested on the girls, all that was left of the vibrant woman who had given birth to them. "How do I tell them their mom isn't coming home?"

Suddenly, the responsibility he had been given seemed even more insurmountable.

Fiona put a plate in front of Sam and sat down with her own. She knew he probably didn't feel like eating anymore, but she needed to do something to be of help.

"Tonight all you need to worry about is getting them home, setting up their portable cribs and getting them to sleep," she said to him. "You've got that down, right?"

Sam nodded and shrugged. "Yeah, shouldn't be too hard."

Carol wiped a tear from her face and lifted her chin.

"She's right. Let's just focus on their care and keeping. Their father should be the one to tell them about Bethany."

Sam frowned. "Was there any news on Ben?"

The older woman shook her head. "No, they are still working on him. He's probably going to be laid up for a long time, though. The best thing you can do is make sure the girls are in a stable situation until he is back on his feet."

Fiona started making a mental checklist of all the food and supplies he would need for at least a week or so watching the kids. Who knows how long they would be with him?

"Okay, the local church has some emergency foster placement bags for just this kind of scenario, with some diapers and baby food. I'll stop by on my way tomorrow to grab you one. We'll go over what else you may need and then take a trip to the store."

Sam's shoulders sank in relief. "You are a lifesaver, you know that?"

His smile warmed her heart. This was why Fiona did this. Not to see families break apart, but to see them come together and do great things despite adversity. Maybe someday she would add Sam and the girls to her stockpile of success stories that she kept next to Nana's.

"Well, first step in your emergency training is getting the kids in their car seats. I can help you if you want, or you can try it on your own and I can step in if you need it," Fiona said.

There were so many times in her line of work that she had buckled little ones into car seats as she removed them from dangerous situations. Every day her job weighed on her. The exposure to so much pain and suffering on a daily basis was difficult. Fiona shook her head to push those thoughts from her mind, focusing all the good she had done in reunifying families and making sure children found a safe home in which to thrive. And now she would help out another family in need—one belonging to her friend.

"I think I can give it a whirl. How hard can it be?" Sam picked up Hazel's car seat from the front hallway and studied it.

Fiona and Carol laughed while finishing their dinner, watching as Sam took each car seat out and struggled to install it in his car.

"You and my grandson seem to be getting along well," Carol said, her voice laced with hints that had Fiona laughing, despite the somber mood from earlier.

"I'm on to you, Carol. I know why you are pushing me and Sam together," she said. "I'm going to help him because he needs it, and those girls need it, but you can get any ideas of anything else between us out of your mind."

Her neighbor scowled playfully. "I don't see why you can't do both. You're single. He's single. It's time you got out there and connected with someone your own age, instead of with me every night."

Fiona squeezed her hand. "I love coming to see you. Besides, I would worry about you if I didn't visit every day."

Carol chuckled. "Oh, you are the sweetest girl. I know you promised your nana you would look out for me, but anyone else would have stopped long ago."

"I told you I enjoy spending time with you."

Carol shook her head. "No, it's more than that. You're very kind, Fiona. And more of the world needs to see it and to be kind back. I see how tired you are when you come home from work each day. How hard that job is on you."

Fiona shrugged. "You knew my grandmother well, so you know that my answer will probably be the same as hers. The rewards far outweigh the negatives. It's all about helping out those families. And I'll help your grandson."

Carol opened her mouth to speak, but Fiona held up a finger. "And no... I'm not interested in dating him."

Her friend sighed. "Why do you always shut down the possibility of any romantic relationship whenever I bring it up?"

Fiona leaned back in her chair, looking at the floor instead of Carol's eyes. "I see so many broken hearts and families every day. Those people were all in love once. And then it fell apart. Those kids were once celebrated, and many of them end up neglected like trash."

Carol gave her a sympathetic smile. "You've become jaded."

"Maybe. I just don't think I could trust any relationship knowing how so many of them end. In pain. And I don't think I could bring children into this world knowing all the terrible things they could encounter."

After making a disgruntled noise, Carol stood up and started packing the girls' toys back in their diaper bag. "I think that someday you'll meet someone that will change your mind about relationships."

Fiona wished she could have the same confidence as

Carol. The thought of dating someone or even getting married made her feel almost ill with nerves.

"And as for bringing children into this world—I think any child of yours would be safe and loved, simply because you were their mama," Carol said.

Her words filled Fiona with warmth, but they did not melt her worries away. "That doesn't stop bad things from happening to them. Look at your great-grandbabies today. They have good parents who loved them and kept them safe, but now they are going through this."

She handed Carol the last of the toys, and the older woman pulled her in for a hug. "We can't protect everyone from bad things, but we can be there to help them make it through. Just like Sam is gonna do for those girls, with your help."

Before she could respond, Sam poked his head back into the kitchen. "I got the car seats in, but…do you think you can help me get the girls buckled? I'm trying to figure out Hannah's buckles, and Hazel keeps undoing hers and climbing everywhere while I'm distracted."

They followed him to the door and laughed at the sight of Hazel jumping up and down in the back seat. Fiona followed him to the car and buckled Hazel in, finding a strap that Sam had missed. She handed her cell phone over to the toddler with a cartoon already playing.

Sam arched an eyebrow at that. "I thought that too much screen time was a bad thing for kids?"

Fiona tickled Hannah's feet as she buckled her in. "You're in survival mode right now, and you have to use every tool in your arsenal. That includes whatever will distract the wild toddler while you buckle in the baby."

Sam ran his fingers through his hair. He looked exhausted. "How am I going to get them upstairs with all their gear and get it set up and put them to bed?"

She patted his arm. "You've got this, remember? One step at a time. Use distraction when you can. And keep your role as the fun uncle. Make a game out of everything you can."

He eyed her warily. "I'll try, but don't be surprised if you walk into chaos tomorrow and none of us have slept."

Fiona chuckled before shutting the car door. "You'll be fine. I'll be there bright and early with supplies. Good night, Sam."

He studied her for a moment before taking a determined breath, squaring his shoulders and crossing to the driver's side. "Night. Fiona. Thanks for everything. And you're right. I've got this."

As he pulled away from Carol's house with children's music blaring over the speaker, Fiona waved at Hazel. She said a silent prayer that they would be all right. She strived to be just like her nana and help whoever was in need. And it looked like she had just gotten her next mission.

Chapter Three

His back hurt.

His neck hurt.

There was a baby drooling on his chest. But Sam didn't dare move a muscle when he woke up the next morning. It had taken him forever to get the girls into bed last night. He downloaded ten books to his e-reader for Hazel and it still wasn't enough. She also demanded several songs and scolded him because he didn't sing them the right way. Toddlers sure got cranky when they were tired.

After the three-year-old's eyes finally started to droop and she fell asleep with her thumb in her mouth, Sam was able to start his own bedtime routine. He was just lying down and closing his eyes when Hannah started to cry.

Several snuggles and a bottle later, she still wouldn't let him put her down and would start fussing each time that he tried. Finally, he gave up and lay on the couch and let his baby niece fall asleep on his chest. He dozed off a few times, too, but he wasn't in a comfortable enough position to get any real rest.

"Unkie! I hungry!"

The sight of Hazel pushing all her blankets and pillows off her portable cot forced him to get up, moving as gently as possible so that he wouldn't wake Hannah. How did parents juggle everything like this?

He put the baby down gently in her crib, sending a prayer of thanks when she didn't wake yet. Sam needed all his free hands to feed her older sister. He didn't really have any kid-friendly food in the house, but she seemed content with some peanut butter toast and orange juice.

"I'm glad we're going shopping today. You can pick out whatever you like to eat best," Sam told her as she grinned happily, her cheeks already covered with food.

"Nuggies!"

He chuckled and pulled out a piece of paper and wrote "chicken nuggets" on the list. There were so many things that he needed that Sam didn't even know where to start. He supposed that he could stop by the hospital and get a key for his brother's house from his parents and pick up clothes, bottles and toys for the girls. But he didn't want to bring them home and upset them because their parents weren't there. Fiona's words yesterday about babies and trauma were resonating with him now.

Just as he thought of Fiona, there was a knock on the door indicating she had arrived to help them for the day.

"You look a little worse for the wear," she said with a vibrant smile. "Rough night?"

Fiona handed him a cup of coffee from his favorite place down the street. "You're a lifesaver. How can you be so chipper in the morning?"

She looked like she ate sunshine for breakfast, actually. He still had a hard time reconciling the stern case-worker he first met with the woman before him. She once again wore casual clothing, loose hair and a bright smile.

Fiona tousled Hazel's hair as she sat down at the kitchen table. "I'm actually a morning person. Also, I didn't have two babies to worry about all night."

She leaned forward with a napkin and wiped the peanut butter off Hazel's face. She made it look so easy. "How are you doing today, pumpkin?"

The little girl picked up his grocery list and handed it to her. "Nuggies, Fi, nuggies."

Sam laughed. "She has a one-track mind. We'll get you some chicken nuggets, Hazel, I promise."

Fiona looked over his list, approving of most of his items, and adding a few suggestions of her own. He was so thankful that she was helping him.

"It might be your instinct to leave them with me and run to the store or have me go get all this for you, but I think that you really just need to dive in and experience the joy of shopping with two little ones along."

He arched an eyebrow at that. "Why do I have a feeling that there is nothing joyful about the experience?"

Fiona grinned. "No comment."

She unloaded everything she brought over, including the foster care emergency kit that had baby clothes and supplies for a few days. It wouldn't be enough to tide the girls over for long, but he was grateful for the help from the community.

Sam was quiet for a second, thinking about his idea from earlier. "Hey, you know how you said I need to be better at asking for help?"

She leaned back and folded her arms, giving him an encouraging look. "I'm all ears. What do you need?"

"Do you think you can watch the girls for a little bit before we go to the store?"

He filled her in on his idea to grab a key and get some of their stuff. "I want to keep them away from the hospital and the whole situation for as long as possible."

Fiona nodded. "That's a really great idea. And it will be good for you to check in with your parents and see your brother in person."

Sam shrugged. "Well, he's unconscious, so it's not like he'll even know I'm there."

"He'll know. Or at least some part of him will. And it will be good for you, too. To see him and know that he's alive."

An ache spread through his chest as he thought of his brother barely surviving the crash yesterday and the loss of his sister-in-law. It still didn't seem real. He was in shock, exhausted and firmly in survival mode with the girls.

"Thank you so much for all your help. I know we only met yesterday, but you're already doing so much for me," Sam said.

Fiona gave Hazel a refill on juice, but diluted it by half with water. "It's easier on her tummy," she said when she noticed Sam watching. "And you're welcome for all the help. To be honest, your grandmother talks about you so much that I feel like I already know you pretty well."

Sam rolled his eyes at that. "She probably started talking about how nice I am, and oh yeah, single, too."

Fiona giggled. "Yeah, that maybe came up a time or

two, but I always told her that I wasn't interested. No offense. I'm just not looking to date anyone right now."

Sam leaned back in his chair with a sigh. "We are on the same page, but I can't get Gran to understand that I'm happy with my life the way it is now. I have a risky job, and I'm not sure I could focus on it if I knew that I had a girlfriend or wife out there worrying about me."

He had seen the stress lines around the eyes of his captain's wife every time they came back from a long call. Sam couldn't ever do that to someone.

"Well, hopefully, she'll get the hint after a while. She just wants you to be happy. Maybe seeing you take care of your nieces will stop her from pressuring you to give her great-grandbabies," Fiona said.

"Hopefully. Oh, and I didn't get to say it to you yesterday, but thank you for all you do to help my grandmother."

Fiona waved away his gratitude. "I wouldn't say that I do much except share dinner with a friend every night."

Sam arched an eyebrow at that. "And fetch her mail, plant flowers in her garden, do light cleaning from time to time, make sure she eats. You do a lot around there. I can't thank you enough."

From the other room, Hannah started to fuss. Sam rose to go get her, while Fiona helped Hazel down from her booster seat. When he returned to the kitchen with the baby, she was already preparing a bottle. Fiona picked up their conversation while she tested the temperature of the milk.

"Truth be told, I love the company. I miss my own nana, and yours has kind of adopted me," Fiona said.

"So I guess that kind of makes these girls my family, too."

His gran was good at loving on people who needed it the most. Still, he couldn't discount all the things that Fiona did for her while he was busy on the job. "You're a better grandkid to her than I am, that's for sure."

Fiona just shook her head. "You really need to have more faith in yourself. Come on, let's get this baby fed and then head to the store. Lots to do today."

"Yeah, Unkie. You. Fi. Nuggies," Hazel chimed in.

Fiona looked up at him with a sparkle in her eyes. "You heard the boss."

As he fed Hannah, he couldn't help but look forward to their shopping trip, as long as Fiona was with them. He really needed to get out of this apartment for some fresh air. And he was starting to enjoy her company, too. She made him feel like he could do this guardian thing.

Hopefully, their shopping trip would go off without a hitch.

The grocery store with a baby and a toddler was an adventure at best, a disaster at worst. Today's outing sat somewhere in the middle.

Fiona couldn't help but giggle at the look of resigned frustration on Sam's face throughout their shopping trip. Hannah kept throwing her pacifier and when he went to grab it, Hazel would add a bunch of stuff to the cart because she was "helping."

Finally, Fiona stepped in and took the toddler to the freezer aisle so that they could find the best chicken nuggets while Sam tackled the rest of the list.

"I don't know what I would have done without you,"

he said, loading the groceries in the back of the car while she buckled the girls in their car seats. "How do parents do this?"

Fiona laughed and handed Hazel the cookie they bought in the bakery as a bribe for good behavior in the checkout lane. "Well, I've heard that curbside pickup has been the greatest invention for parents of small children. But you have to order that ahead of time, and we were kind of in an emergency situation here."

Sam's eyes widened. "I can't believe I didn't think of that. I'm totally going to use that next time."

Fiona couldn't help but admire how well he was handling all this. He could have screamed and run for the hills with the added responsibility. Sure, he had expressed doubts toward his abilities last night, but he had pulled up his bootstraps and handled it like a champ. As much as he liked to, according to Carol, claim he was all about the bachelor's life, he was taking to domesticity very well.

Fiona was about to tell him so once they were both in the car, but her phone rang. She gave Sam an apologetic look. "I'm sorry, it's my work phone. I've got to take this."

Officer Steve Shinn was on the other line, and Fiona set her shoulders, preparing for bad news. "Normally, I would dial the on-call number for your agency, but we worked together at this residence last time and I knew that you would want to be involved."

The two of them worked together on a lot of cases, and Fiona often called him when she needed help. He was always the kindest officer on the force, and he and his wife were foster parents, so they understood the needs of children in some of these difficult circumstances.

"Which family is it?"

Fiona bit back her annoyance at the two parents she had tried to help. Officer Shinn told her that despite the anger management classes that she had required them to take, a violent domestic dispute had broken out at the house today. Thankfully, the children weren't hurt, but they were shaken up, especially since the son had been the one who called the police while he kept his sister upstairs and away from the fight.

"It would probably be best if you came and picked up the kids. Both parents will be spending the rest of the weekend in jail, if not longer," Officer Shinn said. "Probably much longer. It was bad, and this wasn't the first offense for either of them."

Fiona gritted her teeth. She hated breaking up families, but it was clear based on the police report that the home would not be safe for a while. Although the parents didn't harm their children, neither was in a place where they could effectively care for the kids.

She promised the officer that she would be there within the hour, and hung up the phone. "I hate to ask, but do you mind delaying your trip to visit your brother and get the girls' stuff? I have to go do something for work that should take me a few hours. I can be back later this afternoon."

Fiona would much rather spend that time with Hannah and Hazel, but there were two other kids out there who needed her more right now.

"Do I mind? Of course not. You're doing me a huge favor anyway by watching them. Go do what you have to do. We'll hang out and eat chicken nuggets while you're gone," Sam said.

"Nuggies," Hazel chimed in from the backseat.

Fiona gave a halfhearted laugh, and Sam's brows dropped as he glanced at her. "Are you all right?"

She shrugged. "Yeah, I'll be fine. Sometimes my job is just a lot to take. I'm bracing myself for a tough afternoon."

Sam reached over and squeezed her hand. His was warm compared to Fiona's. She didn't realize how much of a chill had gone through her at the phone call. "It takes a really strong and kind person to do what you do. Those kids are so blessed to have you."

They didn't say anything the rest of the trip home, and it was only when she went to get out of the car back at his apartment building that she realized they were still holding hands. Fiona felt her cheeks burn as she quickly pulled away from him.

"I'll help you get the girls up and bring in the groceries before I go," she said.

Sam shook his head. "Nope, I've got this. I need to start learning how to do this stuff on my own because you won't always be here to bail me out."

That was the goal—for him to be able to do this independently. But she liked the idea of spending more time with Sam and his nieces. "Well, I'm not quitting on you anytime soon. I'll be back in a bit."

He reached out his hand toward hers and then stopped himself. "Good luck. I'm going to go lay Hannah down for her nap and then Hazel is going to be my big helper on bringing all this in."

The toddler beamed at them. "I's big help!"

They laughed and Fiona was grateful that her mood was a little lighter when she climbed into her car. She said a prayer on her way to the residence that God would give her the right words and actions to help the kids who waited for her there.

When she pulled up, Officer Shinn was sitting on the porch with six-year-old twins, Abby and Cole. They had tear tracks running down their cheeks, but small smiles as the policeman showed them a video on his phone. He looked up at her when she approached and handed the phone off to Cole.

"Here, buddy. You and your sister watch the rest of the video while I talk with Miss Shay."

They stepped a little distance away from the kids, and the officer gave Fiona a rundown of what happened at the home. "Both parents escalated it too far, so they will probably each see charges, unfortunately. You'll need to take the kids into the state's care for now."

Fiona hated when it came to this, but she needed to make sure the children had a safe home to sleep in. She prayed that the parents would do what they needed to do to reunify their family. If not, Fiona would have to find a forever home for them that was safe. In the meantime, she had to find them an emergency placement and make sure their immediate needs were met—including their emotional ones.

"Come on, guys. Let's go sort through some of your clothes and bring some of your favorite toys with you," Fiona said, trying to keep her voice as cheerful as possible. "I'm going to make sure you're all right."

Cole looked up at her with his face tight and his

fists clenched. "Where's our mommy? What did you do with her?"

Fiona squatted down so that she was on eye level with the kids. This always helped her to make a connection. When they were in this situation, it felt like everyone else was making decisions for them and that they were just chess pieces moving around. Fiona vowed to change that by making each kid feel like they were important.

"Your mom and dad had to go with the police so they could cool down from their fight. They may need to take a while to learn to keep their hands to themselves when they're mad. My job is to make sure that kids are safe, so you're going to have to stay with another nice family for a bit until we make sure everything is okay."

The little girl frowned. "But when do we get to come home? What about my kitty?"

Fiona made a mental note to call a local animal rescue that fostered pets and prayed again that the parents would take all the anger management classes and do all the therapy visits she was sure the judge would require in order to regain custody. "I'm going to make sure your kitty is taken care of. And you, too."

Abby's bottom lip jutted out. "Our mommy didn't hurt us, though. She just hit Daddy. And he punched holes in the wall."

She thanked her heavenly Father that they had not seen or witnessed everything that was mentioned in the report. Fiona pulled the two kids into a hug. "That was pretty scary, huh?"

They both nodded. "Well, let's get you somewhere

less scary for a bit, and then we'll figure out what happens next."

The two kids went inside to grab their clothes. She told them to pack their favorite stuffed animal and blanket. While many foster kids traveled around with a garbage bag as their suitcase and very little stuff, Fiona advocated for each of them to have a bag of their own and all the comfort of home they could bring. If kids didn't have a bag around, she had a stash of duffel bags in her trunk that the church had collected last year.

As Abby and Cole filled their bags, Fiona wandered around the house, making sure everything was shut off that needed to be. There was food cooking on the stove. The fight must have started during dinner. She turned it off.

Sadness filled her when she saw the kids' drawings so lovingly taped to the refrigerator door. There was no doubt that this mother loved her kids. Both parents just needed to regulate their temper a little more. Hopefully, they would get the help they needed.

Fiona entered the living room and held back tears when she saw a large family photo hanging above their fireplace. It was professionally done, with the family in matching outfits, smiling like they didn't have a care in the world.

This was why Fiona didn't believe that happily-ever-afters existed. Behind the smiles and happy photos, there was anger and resentment. She saw it far too often in her job. That picture did not seem to reflect a family on the brink of falling apart.

And yet, it did.

The kids were silent as she drove them to her office.

She knew better than to try to be cheery at a time like this. The best she could do was kindness. And to be a listening ear if they wanted to talk.

"Are you guys hungry?"

The two nodded, so she ran through the drive-through of the local burger place on the way. Judging by the way they stuffed the food into their mouths, it had been a while since they had a full meal. Fiona's heart broke for these little ones.

At the office, one of their volunteers took the kids to the corner that featured toys and coloring books while Fiona dug into their file. Based on the information she had, there were no relatives in state that could take them overnight. They had an aunt and a grandmother who lived farther away, but they would need an emergency foster care placement until they could be picked up by family.

Fiona called Sam to let him know she would be another hour or so to find a placement before she could watch the girls.

"It's all right. You do what you've got to do. We're all good here," he said, but she could hear Hannah crying in the background and Hazel babbling.

"Are you sure? Because it sounds a little chaotic." She tried to hold in her giggle, but it slipped out.

"Yeah, I'm starting to understand that doing anything and going anywhere with two little kids is going to be chaotic. But as you told me today—I've got this."

Fiona couldn't help but smile as she hung up the phone. Despite the terrible situation she was dealing with at work, it was nice to know that she had been able to do some good today regardless.

Sighing, she dove back into finding an emergency

placement. Thankfully, she found someone with two beds open so the kids wouldn't have to be separated. And it was with one of their longest serving foster parents, an elderly couple who had been doing this for decades. Mrs. Wilkins and her homemade chocolate chip cookies may not fix all that broke the kids' hearts today, but perhaps they would make them feel a little better.

But before she took them there, she needed to work on their plan for the future. Fiona sighed as she tracked down the phone number for the aunt. She prayed that the number was still current and that she could get ahold of someone tonight.

"Hello, this is Kyla," a cheerful voice said from the other line. She hated to dim some of that joy, but hopefully, the woman could share some of it with her niece and nephew.

"Hi, this is Fiona Shay with the Colorado Department of Children and Family Services."

There was a groan on the other end of the line. "What did she do now?"

As Officer Shinn had suggested, this apparently wasn't the first time this family had seen trouble.

"Are you the sister of Casey Truitt?"

"Yes, I'm her sister. Are the kids okay?"

Good, she cared about them. They were off to a good start.

"They are fine, but a little shook up. There was a fight between your sister and her husband. Unfortunately, they've been arrested and the kids are being taken into emergency foster care."

The woman gasped. "They don't need to go into foster care. I can take them. I'm out the front door right now."

Fiona wiped a tear from her face as she smiled into

the phone. It was nice to have a family member be so willing to help. Most relatives begrudgingly agreed to help when she called, so this was a breath of fresh air.

"Oh, thank you so much. When do you think you'll arrive?"

The woman hesitated. "I probably won't get there until morning, even if I find a red-eye flight to get on. Are they…"

Fiona rushed to reassure her. "I will make sure they stay with the sweetest couple tonight that will feel like a visit to someone's grandparents, and they will be ready for you in the morning."

The woman's voice shook when she responded. "Thank you so much, for everything. How long do you think it will be this time?"

That told Fiona that she had indeed cared for the kids in this situation before. "I'm afraid it will be a while, due to their previous offenses. I'm so appreciative of you stepping up and being willing to take them."

Her mind went to Sam, who at this very moment was stepping up to the task of caring for his own nieces.

Kyla cried into the phone again. "I begged her. I asked her to please leave the kids with me last time. They didn't deserve all the mess they had been through. They were happy with me, and their life was stable. The last time, they were with me long enough to start kindergarten, make friends. It broke my heart to see them go."

Fiona felt for the woman, who only wanted to help, but lost the connection with the kids when their mother moved them away. At least Sam would still live close to the girls after growing so much closer to them.

"Why did they cross country?" she asked.

Kyla cleared her throat. "As soon as the state agreed to reunify them last time, they picked up and moved, hoping that somewhere else would be better. My sister isn't a bad person, really, she just has this image of a perfect family, but she and her husband aren't able to give that to each other."

Fiona bit her tongue before blurting out that there was no such thing as a perfect family. All anyone could do was the best with what they were given. And love each other and put their care and comfort above their own. But oftentimes, they failed miserably. That was why she was there—to help families and kids pick up the pieces, and rebuild their lives into something better. Whether that was through reunification or by finding a new forever family.

Fiona was so thankful that their aunt was able to care for the kiddos indefinitely until whatever would happen with the parents was decided. She said another prayer for the judge for wisdom in deciding what would be best in this scenario.

An hour later things were settled, and Mrs. Wilkins had their file and was driving them home with promises of a warm bed and yummy snacks. Fiona had a newly colored picture to hang on her wall from each of the kids. She texted Sam again to let him know she was on her way.

He surprised her by calling her back immediately.

"Sam, is everything okay?"

"Yeah, but I'm glad you're on your way," he said, his voice sounding breathy with excitement. "My parents just called. I need to get to the hospital. Benjamin's awake."

Chapter Four

Sam paced his apartment, waiting for Fiona to arrive. He was anxious to see his brother, just to know that he was going to be all right. And to be there for his parents. The girls were making a game of pacing with him—Hazel skipping behind him and Hannah crawling along, laughing as if this was the best game ever.

Finally, there was a knock on the door and all three of them hurried over to answer it. Fiona looked tired as she walked in, and another wave of guilt flooded Sam for leaving this responsibility on her after her already long day.

"I'm so sorry to ask this of you after your call. Are you sure you're up for it? I can try to throw myself at the mercy of one of the guys from work to sit with them, or bring them with me," Sam said.

Fiona sank down on the couch. "I'm fine. We'll be okay here for a while, watching some cartoons, eating some snacks. It's time we had a proper girls' night."

She winked at Hazel and the little one hopped up and down with excitement. "Girls only, Unkie. You go."

Sam chuckled. "Well, I know where I'm not welcome. But seriously, call me if you need me to come back or anything…"

She rolled her eyes at him and practically shoved him out the door to go visit his brother.

"We're fine. Go see Benjamin."

It was amazing that someone he had just started to get to know for the first time yesterday had already become such an essential part of his life. Sam didn't know how he would survive without Fiona's help at this point. The girls were thrilled to see her. Hazel even shared some of her beloved chicken nuggets as the two of them curled up on the couch to watch cartoons.

He couldn't tear his gaze away from the two of them; something about the scene made him feel lighter. Probably just the sweetness of it all, and knowing Hazel and Hannah would be well cared for. Nothing more.

The drive to the hospital seemed to pass quickly as he braced himself to face whatever he would find inside his brother's room. His dad had warned him that Benjamin was still in critical condition and not able to communicate well.

When he walked into the busy lobby, Sam was surprised to see his father there to greet him. The normally strong and confident man looked like he had the weight of the world on his shoulders. He pulled Sam in for a big bear hug.

"It's so good to see you, son. It's been a long twenty-four hours," his dad said.

Sam couldn't believe it had only been that long since the accident rocked their world. It felt like much longer.

"Are you all right? Did you guys get any sleep? Do you need any food?"

His father gave him a small smile as he guided Sam toward the elevator. "You don't need to worry about us. We're hanging in there. It's so much better now that he's awake."

His father explained that the surgery had gone well and they were able to repair most of the damage to Benjamin's organs, but he still had a long road of recovery ahead of him. "On top of all that, he has several broken bones. He's going to be here for a long time."

"And did you tell him about Bethany?" Sam asked, bracing himself to hear about the hard conversation that must have been.

Dad's eyes filled with tears. "Yeah, and that broke him all over again. I think he wished he was back asleep and didn't know what was going on."

Sam wiped his own tear away. "I wish I knew how to talk to him. To help him."

His dad laid a hand on his shoulder. "He's hurting, son, both physically and emotionally. It's going to take a lot of time and love to heal both."

Sam knew the accident was bad, but it sounded like Benjamin's survival was a miracle. "Well, I will take care of the girls until he's ready for them."

He would have to ask around for a babysitter to watch the kids while he worked, though. Sam couldn't stay out indefinitely. That was a worry for later, though.

"How are my granddaughters? Are they asking about their mom and dad?"

They had decided not to tell the girls yet about their parents, because they were too young to understand.

Maybe he could bring them to visit their dad in the hospital and he could explain that they would be staying with him until they could go home together.

"So far, so good. I let Hazel pick out some of her favorite foods from the store so she's a happy camper right now. I'm going to stop on my way home and pick up some of their clothes and toys so they'll feel more comfortable," Sam explained.

His father's shoulders slumped in relief. Dave Tiernan was a man who loved his family wholeheartedly. Sam only wished he could take more stress away from him during this time.

"Who's watching the girls now?"

Sam stepped into the elevator and waited as his dad punched in the button for the fourth floor before answering. "A friend who has been helping me out. Her name is Fiona."

It would probably be accurate to describe Fiona as a friend at this point. They had shared the world's worst soup and survived the grocery store with babies. If that didn't form a fast friendship, what else could?

His dad's eyebrows went up. "Fiona Shay? Your gran's neighbor?"

Sam turned his head quickly at the words. "Yeah. Do you know her?"

"I've met her several times. She does a lot for your gran since we can't get out there every day. A good woman."

Sam smiled. "That she is. She's really been a lifesaver since yesterday."

His dad looked at him thoughtfully. "You know, your gran has talked a lot about setting the two of you up. You could do worse."

Sam groaned. "Really, Dad? We're at the hospital with a family tragedy and you're joining Gran's matchmaking campaign?"

His father chuckled. "To be honest, it's a nice distraction. It's been a long night."

"Sorry to disappoint, but there is nothing going on between Fiona and me other than friendship. We only met yesterday, and she's just helping out. You know that I'm not interested in a relationship right now."

As they approached the fourth floor, his father nudged Sam on the shoulder. "Well, maybe spending some time with your nieces might have you wanting a family of your own."

Sam rolled his eyes. "They are my family."

"You know what I mean. Your own kids. A wife. Someone to come home to each day. That has to have some appeal, right?"

They stepped into the hospital wing and toward the ICU. "Don't count on it. I slept only about two hours last night. I don't know how parents do this all the time."

When they opened the room, his father took a deep breath as he gazed at Benjamin in the bed and then back to Sam. "It's worth it. Every hour spent raising you boys was a gift from God."

His voice choked up with the words, and Sam pulled his father in for a hug. A hand rubbed along Sam's back, a smaller one than his father's. He turned to see his mother there, her eyes also shining with tears. "There's my boy. Let me hold you for a minute."

He completely understood where she was coming from. With one son's life in danger, she wanted to hold on to the other one as tightly as she could. He didn't mind one bit.

"How are you holding up, Mom?"

Sam leaned back and took a good look at her. There were bags under her eyes and her entire countenance exuded weariness.

"I'm okay, love. Just worried about Ben. Thanks for watching Hannah and Hazel. I know it must be hard for them to be away from home. And without their mama…"

She broke out into sobs again, and Sam hugged her tighter. His dad put an arm around them both. "I'm going to take her outside so she doesn't upset Ben. You go have a talk with your brother. I think it might do him some good to see you."

Sam nodded and turned to walk to the other side of the room, where his brother was staring out the window. His father laid a hand on his arm to stop him. "He's…not in a good place right now. Just giving you a fair warning."

That was probably an understatement. The man had lost his wife and almost died. He would be a mess as well. Sam felt like that anyway, and he wasn't even the one in the hospital bed.

Looking over at his brother, he held back a gasp as he studied him more closely. Benjamin's face was a myriad of colors as bruises peppered every visible inch of skin. The rest of him was a mix of casts and bandages. He was hooked up to an IV and several monitors. He wouldn't be moving for a while. Benjamin was so still that if Sam didn't know better, he might think he was asleep.

He approached Ben slowly, steeling himself to see his brother in pain. Sam knew he had to be the strong one right now.

"Hey, man. It's good to see you awake."

Ben gave no indication that he even heard Sam's words. He just kept looking out the window with a vacant expression on his face. Sam closed his eyes and said a prayer, not only for healing for his brother, but also that he would know the right things to do and say to help ease his emotional pain.

"The girls are doing well," Sam said as he pulled a chair closer to the bed. "I think I finally got the hang of cleaning up Hannah without her making a run for it."

Still no response from Benjamin.

"Hazel roped me into buying so many packages of chicken nuggets. There's no way she's going to be able to get through them all before you bring her home."

His brother blinked at that, and frowned. "She's not coming home." His voice was hoarse but hard and determined.

Sam dropped his jaw.

"What?" Sam was so thankful Benjamin finally spoke that he didn't process his words.

"They can't come home to that house. Not without Bethany there. Not with me there. I'm not the person who should ever be in charge of caring for them again."

Sam couldn't believe the words coming out of his brother's mouth. Ben was always the strong one between the two of them. The steady, solid older brother that he always leaned on in need. How could he even think that he wouldn't be able to care for his daughters? "What do you mean? You're their father!"

Benjamin turned to look at him, his gaze no longer unfocused but angry. His eyes were narrowed and his jaw tight. "And what a father I am. It's my fault they lost the one person who could care for them best."

Sam's heart broke at his brother's words. "Ben, no. This was an accident. And the police said it was the other driver's fault. You can't hold yourself responsible…"

His brother looked away out the window again. His countenance was blank once more, with a look that Sam now recognized as despair. "Just go. Take care of my daughters. You'll do a better job than I ever could."

Sam's brows furrowed in confusion. "I will watch them until you are ready to be their dad again. And that day will come. You just need to heal first."

Ben was quiet for a moment, and Sam wondered if he was ending the conversation. "I won't ever be ready. I can't keep them alive. I couldn't save Beth."

Sam sighed. "Ben…"

"Just go!"

His brother's shout startled him because he had spoken so softly and with effort within the past few minutes. Their dad rushed in and was at the bedside within seconds. The monitors were beeping wildly. "Calm down, son. Your heart rate is getting too high."

Ben's jaw tightened. "I want him to go. I don't want to talk about the girls anymore."

Their mother slipped into the other side of the bed and wiped hair off Ben's forehead. "It's all right, honey. Sam just wanted to make sure you were doing okay. And to let you know the girls were cared for. He's going to go right now."

Knowing he had been dismissed, Sam backed out of the room. His heart hurt after the exchange. Ben had never been so cold to him. He knew that his brother loved him, but it still hurt to see that he was causing him to get so upset. Ben was in a bad place emotionally right now, but it didn't make sense that he was avoiding mention of his own daughters. Those two little girls would make anyone smile. How could he not want to see or talk about them?

Sam didn't realize he was pacing in the corridor until his father stepped out of the room and he almost ran into him. "I'm sorry, Dad. I didn't mean to upset him."

The elder man leaned against the wall and closed his eyes. "It wasn't you. He's been like this all morning. From the moment he heard about the loss of his wife, he's blamed himself for the accident and keeps saying that it should have been him that died instead of Bethany."

Tears formed in Sam's eyes. He grieved the loss of his sister-in-law, but he hated the idea of his brother taking her place. "I thought it was the other driver's fault? My captain said he crashed into them."

His father grimaced. "Yeah, he did and is in a coma just down the hall there. But Benjamin said he and Beth were arguing and he thinks that it distracted him."

Sam frowned. "And he believes that if they hadn't been arguing, the accident wouldn't have happened?"

One thing he saw often on his job was people playing the game of "what if?" What if they hadn't left that candle burning? What if they had made something else for dinner, bought a different brand of Christmas lights, etc.? He believed that focusing on what one could have done differently never changed the situation at hand.

His father sighed. "No matter how hard we try to tell him otherwise, we can't get it in his head. He doesn't want to face the girls because he just keeps saying that he killed their mother."

Sam closed his eyes, processing what was happening. It seemed that it wasn't only his brother's body that needed to heal, but his heart, too. "I'll keep them as long as he needs me to."

His father was quiet for a moment. "As of right now, he wants that to be forever. I'm praying that he comes around, but you need to be prepared for him to not take them for a very long time."

Could he care for his nieces indefinitely? This was not the kind of life he wanted for himself, but he couldn't just abandon them. Hazel and Hannah needed him. Besides, he had Fiona's support now. "Then they will have a home with me until he's ready."

His dad let out a breath and laid a hand on his shoulder. "For what it's worth, I'm really proud of you."

Sam held back the tears that threatened at his father's words. He would forever be a little kid when it came to spending time with this man. Knowing his dad was proud of him gave him an extra boost of motivation to do this caretaking thing right.

When he got back to his truck, he took several moments to gather himself before starting it up and heading to his brother's house. Still, his shoulders remained tight from tension during the visit. Entering the home was surreal. A once lively house now sat still, silent and devoid of any life. He wondered if it would ever be filled with laughter and love again.

Lord, please heal what's going on in my brother's heart. Help him be the dad those girls need, Sam offered up in silent prayer as he gathered toys and clothes in a bag to bring to his apartment. He was affirmed in his decision not to bring his nieces here. It would only serve to remind them what was missing. It was best to keep this as a fun adventure for them for now.

Sam made sure he gathered some of their favorite blankets off the bed, and some extras so he and Hazel could maybe make a blanket fort later. As he gathered the last of their things and locked up the house, he breathed a sigh of relief. Sam wouldn't be back here for a while. It was too much.

Each mile he drove to get back to Hannah, Hazel and Fiona felt like the stress of the day was slipping away. He looked forward to Hannah's chubby hands squishing his cheeks and giggling while he made funny faces. Sam loved when Hazel tried to boss him around like she owned the place. And Fiona…the calm amidst the storm. They were all exactly what he needed to feel better.

When he took his weary steps up the stairs to the apartment, Hazel opened the door and ran out to wrap herself around his leg. "Unkie! You here!"

Looking down at the little girl beaming at him, his resolve strengthened to do everything he could to make their lives happy for as long as he could. Sam may not have wanted the domestic life, but that was what he had now. He just had to figure out how to do it.

When Fiona greeted him with a smile, he noticed

that she looked a little tired. A twinge of guilt went through him when he remembered that she had a rough time at work this afternoon and had still come to sit with the girls.

"Thank you so much for watching them. I'm sorry it took so long."

Fiona shook her head and pulled a covered plate out of the fridge for him. "Don't even worry about it. How is your brother?"

Sam tightened his jaw. "Not great. He's so broken. Both in body and spirit."

She gave a hum of sympathy before putting his food into the microwave. "I can only imagine. I'm sorry your whole family is going through this."

Fiona's kind eyes welcomed him to open up, so he did just that, explaining everything that happened in the hospital. She leaned with her back against the counter and listened without interrupting.

"So it looks like I'm going to be their guardian for a long time. I'm going to have to start looking at daycare options tomorrow."

Fiona opened her mouth to talk, but the microwave beeped. She hopped up and pulled something out, grinning as she placed a plate of lasagna in front of him. He eyed it dubiously…not wanting to insult her but a little afraid to try her cooking again. She just laughed and handed him a fork. "Don't worry, I didn't make it. Someone from the church dropped it by. In fact, they have a whole sign-up list that's filled with people who are going to bring you meals every day, around your work schedule, of course."

Sam's eyes widened at that. "Really? Why would they

go to so much trouble for me and two little babies? We don't eat much," he said before proving himself wrong by diving into the plate of food. The warm meal filled him up. Maybe there was really something to be said about the concept of comfort food.

Fiona grinned. "Your family is well loved, especially your gran. People want to help, but they know there isn't much they can do other than feed you. There's also a schedule to visit your parents at the hospital and to make sure they get a good meal every day."

That was so kind. He had lived in this community his whole life and had volunteered for stuff like this in the past, but he had never been on the receiving end. "Wow, that's… I don't even know what to say."

Fiona laughed and stood up, opening the freezer. "That's not all. There have been so many families from the fire station that have come by to tell you that they are here for you…and they loaded your freezer with food, too. And there are tons of diapers as well. One of the firefighters' wives organized a diaper drive."

That would save him several emergency trips to the grocery store with the girls in tow. He sat there with his eyes wide, but Fiona seemed to understand. "You're not in this alone, Sam. Your whole community is here to help you."

For the first time since yesterday, Sam felt himself relax. It would be a long road ahead for his family, but maybe with the help of their friends, they would be all right. "Thank you…for being here today, and for handling all of this."

Fiona shrugged. "It's part of my job to support families in need. And it's nice to help my family for once.

I love your gran and she loves you. That means we're family, too."

Tomorrow was Sunday, and then after that she would be back to work and not be able to spend her days bailing Sam out with the girls anymore. "We're going to miss you on Monday."

She chuckled. "You're in this for the long haul. I'm not going to abandon you just because I have to work. I'll stop by in the evening and help for as long as I can. And I'll bring a plate of some of this donated food to your gran every night so she still gets fed. Truth be told, it will be a nice break from my cooking."

Sam grinned. "Well, then it's a win-win for everyone."

And suddenly, it felt like everything was going to be fine.

Chapter Five

Exhausted after her long day helping Sam and going in for a work emergency, Fiona slept longer than expected the next morning. She felt bad because she had promised she would be over to start the toddler-proofing process in his apartment. Hazel was bound to get over the excitement of a sleepover soon and start poking around some places that were not kid friendly. Not to mention how fast Hannah moved when she crawled.

But the idea of another day doing nothing but projects around the apartment didn't seem appealing. They needed some fun to boost their moods. Sam had looked so despondent yesterday when he got back from the hospital. And removing kids from their home when she went into work hadn't helped lighten her stress, either.

"What do you think, buddy? Should we go up the mountain?"

Sherlock's head picked up at those words and he ran to the door and stood under the hook where she hung his leash. He may not be energetic when she came home anymore, but that dog loved to go on walks. She often took him up one of the easy trails at the nearby mountain park on the weekends. Fiona hadn't been planning to go today because of everything that happened with Sam, but maybe a little fresh air was what they all needed.

She followed an excited Sherlock to the car and sent Sam a quick text before she pulled out.

On our way. Get the girls dressed and ready to spend some time outdoors.

He sent her back a question mark and she laughed.

Just trust me, she replied.

When she pulled into his apartment complex, Sam was waiting on his front stoop with his nieces.

"Wow, you're getting really good at this childcare thing. They even have their shoes on and everything. From what I've heard, those little things go missing all the time," she teased.

Sam passed her the baby while he helped Hazel into the car seat. "Would you believe that this one did almost all the getting ready by herself? She was so excited to see her best friend Fi."

Fiona observed the mismatched socks and the backward shirt. It was wild, but she loved it. "I can see that. I'm happy to see you, too, pumpkin."

But Hazel ignored her completely because it seemed like she had a new best friend. Sherlock now sat between the two car seats and was greeting the toddler with continuous kisses. Hazel giggled loudly. Sam beamed at her as he got into the car. "That's the best sound in the world, especially after the week we've had."

Fiona directed him to drive to the nearby mountain reserve park, and he arched an eyebrow at that. "Really? A mountain, with babies?"

She rolled her eyes. "You said you would trust me. I know what I'm doing. We all need a little adventure today."

They pulled into the park, and it was already filled with lots of families who were enjoying the sunny weather.

"I brought a picnic lunch. I put the cooler in your trunk while you were loading the girls in their seats. We can have it when we come down from our hike," Fiona said.

Sam turned to her with wide eyes. "You're serious about hiking with two little ones?"

She nodded. "There's an easy trail over there. My nana used to take me up it when I was a girl. It's even safer now. They've paved half of it. And there's a little waterfall with a pond at the end. Plenty of families take this."

He still looked concerned, so she pulled her secret weapon out of her bag.

It was a tangle of canvas and straps and Sam eyed it curiously.

"What is that thing? And why are you letting it near the children? It looks dangerous."

Fiona burst out into laughter at the expression on his face. "It's for Hannah. It's a baby carrier."

He arched an eyebrow at that. "You want me to put my precious baby niece in that thing? No way!"

Fiona rolled her eyes. "It's safe, I promise. I'll help you get it on. My friend swears by it."

Reluctantly, he held out his arms so she could help him.

"I borrowed this from my coworker who had a baby a few years ago. It was a lifesaver. You just strap this around you like a really secure backpack, but on your front, and Hannah can enjoy the hike with you," Fiona said.

Understanding dawned on him as the thing took shape, and a slow smile filled his face. He had dimples…the same ones she had seen on Hazel. It must be a family trait.

It took the two of them a few minutes to figure the contraption out due to their lack of experience, but soon they had Hannah babbling happily, strapped to Sam's chest. Hazel held Fiona's hand as they started the trail.

"That picnic lunch might actually be dinner," Sam muttered as their three-year-old hiking companion stopped to pick up another leaf to examine.

Fiona laughed. "She's exploring her world. This is good for her."

It was taking them an excessively long time to get to the end of the trail, but they were in no hurry. They just let the little girl have the time of her life.

"So why did you choose social work? Other than the obvious fact that you're amazing with kids. I know it's an emotionally difficult job," Sam said as they followed their tiny leader up the trail.

"If my parents had their way, I would be doing something more glamorous and financially rewarding, for sure. I guess that makes me quite the rebel," Fiona said. Not a week went by when she didn't get a request from her mom to come home and give up the life she had built here. But that wasn't going to happen.

"So what sent you down your own path?" he asked again.

Fiona chuckled as Hazel tried to throw a pebble down a slope, but it only made it two feet. She carefully walked near the little girl so that she didn't stray into a dangerous area. "Well, there were several reasons. First and foremost, my nana. She was a social worker and I always wanted to be like her when I grew up. She was so kind and caring."

Sam smiled at her. "Well, you have that part down."

Her cheeks turned pink at his words. To get over her embarrassment, she hurried to continue the conversation.

"Uh...thanks. So anyway, then I met a girl in high school that was in the foster care system. Her placement then was amazing, but she had so many stories about how bad things had been in her original home life, and with some of her previous foster parents. It broke my heart."

Sam gave her a small smile. "And you wanted to change the world?"

She shrugged. "I guess. Or at least a little part of it. There are so many kids out there that just need someone to care."

He nudged her gently. "And you're that person."

Fiona thought of all the lives she had encountered

through the years. So many children in pain. So many broken families. "I try. Some problems are too big to fix, and you just have to be there to support someone as they walk through it."

They took a break at one of the trail benches to have water and granola bars. Hannah wanted down from her carrier, but there was no way they were going to let her crawl around at this height.

"You've been an incredible support for me, and I'm an adult. I can only imagine how much help you are to those kids," Sam said.

Fiona was so used to her parents talking down about what she did that it was lovely to hear someone do just the opposite. She didn't do her job for the praise, however. "Thanks, but I only wish I could do more. The system is so broken at times."

She pushed the momentary melancholy that flooded her away, determined to not think about work and enjoy her day off. "Let's talk about something else. Pizza toppings! Pineapple—yes or no?"

Sam gave her a sideways look and she knew he was onto her about changing the conversation, but he let it go. "Pineapple, yes. But I have to be in a mood for it."

"I'll accept that answer," Fiona said as she stood to start walking again. "Hazel, sweetheart, are your legs getting a little tired?"

Hazel's bottom lip trembled. "I'm a big girl."

Fiona tucked one of the girl's locks that had come loose from her ponytail back behind her ear. "Even big girls get tired. Besides, we want to beat your uncle up this mountain. I need the best person on my team."

The little girl sized up Sam. "Yeah, Hannah not help him at all."

Getting the toddler on Fiona's back was easy, but she was heavier than she looked. "Oof. I'm going to be feeling this in my legs tomorrow."

Sam gave her a sympathetic look. "Do you want to switch kids?"

She gave an exaggerated gasp. "You hear that, Hazel? He's trying to steal you from me. We won't let you defeat us, you nefarious villain!"

Hazel giggled and clung tightly to Fiona's chest. "Yeah, Unkie. We gonna beat you! Go, horsie, go!"

Fiona didn't have to be told twice, hurrying ahead of Sam and Hannah, but mindful to watch of any obstacles that might appear on the trail. She was going to get a workout today, but hearing Hazel's laugh as they raced up the mountain was worth it.

The two ladies did indeed defeat Sam and Hannah to the end of the trail, doing a little victory dance while they waited for him to catch up. He laughed at the sight, giving Hazel a big sloppy kiss on her cheek as a reward.

Fiona couldn't wipe the grin off her face. This was the best day off she'd had in a long time, maybe in forever.

When they got to the top of the trail, he realized that Fiona had been right; it wasn't that difficult a climb at all. He was barely winded, even though he was carrying Hannah on his chest. Maybe that was because of the frequent stops with Hazel. She wanted to explore every inch of the trail, and Fiona had kept up with her to make sure she was safe.

This is fun. I could get used to doing something like this every weekend. He had clung to the solo life for so long, but spending a day out in nature with another adult and two kids wasn't that bad. He was even having more fun than he would be with a TV marathon on his couch and a frozen pizza. That would have been his typical day off.

The waterfall at the top of the trail was more of a drizzle because they hadn't had rain in a long time. Still, the little pond was there, and Hazel squealed in delight and immediately picked up small rocks and began throwing them in so she could hear the plunking sound.

"Here, I'll take the baby for a bit. You play with her," Fiona said, pulling Hannah out of her carrier.

Sam felt another wave of affection for the woman who had helped him so much in the past few days. She seemed to always know what he needed. It was amazing.

He and Hazel spent time trying to find the best rocks to throw in the pond. He tried to show her how to skip rocks like his dad had taught him, but she was a little young for that and didn't have the patience for it. Instead, she just kept plopping them in and giggling at the sound they made. Maybe when they were older, Benjamin could bring them back here and teach both girls to skip rocks properly. Sam sighed, thinking of his brother's emotional turmoil.

Sam shook his head from those thoughts, not wanting to dwell on the negative on such a great day. "I've lived here my whole life and never been up this trail," he said.

Fiona smiled wistfully, closing her eyes as the wind rustled her hair.

She's beautiful, Sam thought, wondering why he hadn't really noticed before. In the station, she had been prim and proper, but out here, in the wild, she looked like she belonged.

"I insisted my grandmother bring me up here when I was a kid and my family came to visit. It was our favorite spot," Fiona explained.

"I can see why."

Hazel ran over and put a rock in Sam's hand. "Round one!"

He made a big show of studying it carefully. "You're right. This one is perfect for skipping. Great find!"

He threw it and it skipped three times. Hazel squealed with excitement. "Again! Again!"

"Okay, well, then go find me another perfect rock."

She ran off on her mission, the adults chuckling as they watched her.

"This is really fun. I come here on my day off every weekend, but I haven't been with other people in a while."

He arched a brow at that. "You've not brought any of your friends up here?"

She giggled. "Your gran wouldn't make it with her cane."

Sam rolled his eyes. "I didn't mean Gran, I meant your other friends."

Fiona looked away. "I don't have a lot of friends outside of work. And none of us from the office have the energy to hang out much after the long days we've had."

He tilted his head, confused. "But you don't hang out with anyone else? Like from church or other friends?"

She shook her head. "Nah, most of the people I know from church are married and have kids. And on the weekend I just kind of want to chill and not really talk to people, you know? I have lived here for a few years, but haven't put in much effort to make friends. So it's my own fault."

He pushed himself off the rock he was leaning against and crossed to her. He reached out a hand, pulling her up straight, too. Hannah babbled cheerfully between them as Sam smiled down at them, shaking Fiona's hand. "Well, allow me to introduce myself. I'm Sam Tiernan, officially your friend."

He had no idea how isolating her job had been. His work friends were more like his family and he had lived here his entire life. Sam knew just about everyone in this town, but he had more than enough room for one more friend in his life. Especially one as kind and giving as Fiona.

Her eyes sparkled as she shook his hand back. "Nice to meet you, friend."

He was reluctant to let her hand go, but had to when Hannah dove toward him and wrapped her arms around his neck.

Fiona laughed. "You are her favorite person now, I guess."

Hazel brought another rock, but this time Fiona gave an attempt to skip it. She failed, laughing as it didn't even make one jump. Hazel's face scrunched up. "Bad rock."

Fiona shook her head. "No, that was the perfect rock. Just a bad throw."

Sam spent the next hour helping Fiona learn the art of rock skipping and helping Hazel find the perfect ones to use. He had never had more fun in his life. Reluctantly, they turned to go back down the trail.

"You know, now that we're officially friends, I think that I will come up here with you whenever I have a weekend off. My days off don't always fall on Saturday or Sunday, but when they do, I'll join you."

Her cheeks turned a lovely shade of pink at that. "You don't have to. I'm fine on my own, or well, with just Sherlock."

The dog in question took that moment to shake its wet fur, drenching all of them with pond water. Fiona yelped and hid behind Sam when he started to do it again. Hazel just put her arms up and enjoyed the water. *Yeah, this was a good day*, he thought with a smile. His good mood continued until they were almost to the bottom when disaster struck.

It happened like it was in slow motion. Hazel's foot caught on a rock and she flew forward. Sam tried to reach for her, but it was too late. The toddler's body lifted into the air and she face-planted on the cement of the trail.

The toddler didn't move or cry, which was terrifying. "Hazel," Fiona cried, rushing forward.

"No, let me check her," he said, handing Hannah off to her. His training as an EMT kicked in. While he was worried as an uncle, he had to remain calm and assess the situation.

He flipped her over gently and his heart caught at the sight of Hazel's face covered in blood. He knew head injuries tended to bleed worse than most, but it was still a startling vision. Her eyes were open and wide with fear. She wasn't crying, but he assumed it was because of the shock.

"You okay, baby girl?"

Her bottom lip quivered as she shook her head.

Something appeared in his line of sight. Fiona was handing him a first-aid kit that she must have carried in her backpack. She really did think of everything.

"Let Unkie check out your owie, okay?"

Hazel gave a nod, her eyes finally pooling with tears.

"Does your head hurt?"

Another nod.

"Anywhere else?"

She pointed to her knee and he saw that had been skinned in her fall as well. "Oh, my. We'll get a bandage on that one, too. Can you move your arms and legs for me really quick, and wiggle your fingers?"

Hazel did as he asked, and he was relieved to see that her injuries were just the cut on her forehead and the scrape on her knee.

"Her eyes aren't dilated, so I think she doesn't have a concussion. She'll be okay."

He heard Fiona's sigh of relief behind him. "But what about all that blood?"

He pulled out some of the antiseptic wipes from the first-aid kit and started cleaning the wound. "It's deep, but I don't think enough that she'll need stitches. I'll bandage it and if it gets worse, we can bring her to the ER for more care."

Hazel was crying in earnest now, but Sam was gentle as he cleaned her wound and put on a bandage. He even put a kiss on it for good measure, something he never did in the field when he treated injuries, but this situation called for it.

"Now, you were such a brave girl. You deserve a reward."

Hazel wiped at her face at that, dirt smudges now smeared with her tears. "Nuggies?"

His heart melted. He would buy her all the chicken nuggets in the world if it made her feel better.

"Yes, we can even get them in a kids' meal with a toy."

Hazel miraculously rebounded at that announcement, hopping to her feet. "Unkie, can't walk. My knee is ouchy. Up!"

She lifted her arms, demanding to be carried. Fiona let out a big laugh from behind them. "By all means, carry the survivor off the mountain. I have Hannah."

And with that, he lifted Hazel off the ground and put her on his shoulders. She giggled with delight and held on tightly to his hair for balance. It stung his scalp, but the sound of her happiness was worth it.

Chapter Six

Fiona watched Sam and Hazel march their way down the rest of the trail and toward the car, singing one of her favorite songs.

He's really good at this. I wonder why he shies away from wanting a family, she thought.

Even though they had been planning a picnic, they instead headed to the nearest fast food place to give Hazel her chicken nuggets. Sometimes a change in plans was worth it.

They ate outside the restaurant so Sherlock could join them. Hazel got an ice cream cone after lunch, and when she got full, she gave the rest to Sherlock. They were best friends now, and he barely gave Fiona a second look all day.

Not that she could blame him; ice cream had staggering bribery powers. When they approached Sam's apartment, her mood dropped, however.

She had so much fun today that Fiona didn't want it to end. She dreaded heading home to her empty house and getting up to go back into work tomorrow. Spending time with Sam and the girls was the first weekend in forever she remembered having fun.

Sam kept glancing at her out the sides of his eyes, and she wondered what he was thinking.

"I know you probably need to go home and do some stuff, but…do you want to come in and help with bath and bedtime?"

Fiona's heartbeat sped up. Either he didn't want the day to end, either, or he just needed her help. It didn't matter, because she would get to stay. "That sounds great. I'm an excellent lullaby singer."

He grinned. "Perfect. With your singing, and my amazing bedtime story skills, we'll have these little ones asleep in no time."

Bath time with two babies proved trickier than either was expecting. More water ended up on the adults and the bathroom floor than stayed in the tub. And Hannah's ninja-like crawling escapes were even worse. It turned out that it was really hard to catch a wet, slippery baby.

By the time they had the girls in their pajamas, they were exhausted and their stomachs hurt from laughing so hard.

"I feel like I've just survived a war," Sam said.

Fiona giggled because his clothes were soaked and his hair was sticking out of place all over his head. "You look like it, too."

He arched an eyebrow at that. "Thanks a lot. I was being kind and not mentioning how you looked right now."

Fiona sputtered at him as she reached up to try to straighten her hair. Sam surprised her by tucking a tendril behind her ear. "I think you look fine. Although slightly drenched."

She gathered her things, getting ready to go, but Sam grabbed them out of her hands and put them back on the table. "What are you doing?"

"After that ordeal, I should probably feed you," Sam said. "Do you want to stay for dinner?"

Fiona knew she should probably say no, that she was spending too much time with him. It would be hard to part ways when he didn't need her anymore. But she couldn't bring herself to walk out the door and go home to her empty house.

She looked over at Sherlock, who was curled up on the living room rug like he belonged there. "I suppose that I could stay for a while."

Sam gave her a grin that made her stomach do a little flip, and led her to the kitchen.

"I'm afraid that all I can offer you is a casserole that someone brought over or chicken nuggets."

He cringed at the latter, and she couldn't help but agree. They had their fill of Hazel's favorite food for a while.

"Or you could save all that casserole for another time and we could try to make something. How are you in the kitchen?"

The wide-eyed expression on his face made her giggle. "I meant the two of us, together. I can't mess it up too much if you're supervising me."

Sam shrugged. "I'm not that much of an expert in the kitchen, either, but I've managed to make an omelet or two while on a long shift at the station."

He went over to the fridge and pulled out some peppers, onions and mushrooms they had bought the other day while at the store together.

"How are your chopping skills?" he asked as he handed her a knife and cutting board.

"Now, that, I can do."

Sam put on some music and they fell into a rhythm in the kitchen. Fiona chopped ingredients while he scrambled the eggs and got the stove ready. She was surprised how easy spending time with him was outside of just taking care of the kids.

This was so different from the first impression she had of him during her training sessions with Sam and his colleagues on the Safe Baby drop protocol.

"Can I ask you a question?"

He paused his movements and looked up at her with an arched brow. "Sure, what is it?"

"Why were you so rude to me the times we met in the past?"

The firefighters at the station were an unruly bunch whenever she gave her presentations. They made peanut gallery comments the entire time.

The corners of his mouth turned up a bit. "I wasn't trying to be mean. I was only teasing."

She frowned at him. "Teasing is only fun when it involves both parties. Otherwise, it's just rude."

He considered her for a moment. "You're right. I'm sorry. I guess the mood at the station is all joking around when we're not on a call and I let myself treat you the same way. I'm sorry."

Fiona shrugged. "I know I should have loosened up a bit if I wanted to connect with your team, but it's hard for me to do that when I'm in work mode."

He resumed his cooking, putting the eggs into the pan and grabbing the ingredients from her. "I get it. Your job deals with a lot of serious stuff, and unruly firefighters probably didn't make your day less stressful."

She shook her head and laughed. "That and I never seem to be able to pin you all down for one meeting."

Sam slid the first omelet on the plate. Fiona had to admit that it looked delicious.

"Yeah, even though this is a small town, they keep us pretty busy," he said. "It's been growing since more and more people from the city are moving out here and commuting."

It was the same at her job. More development and houses meant more families they interacted with. Their workload was growing, but their staff wasn't. "Will they expand the fire department?"

"I hope so. We definitely could use another engine and a bigger crew, but it will probably be a while until the taxes catch up with the needs of the public."

Fiona sighed. That would probably also be the case in her already underfunded department.

"My turn to ask a question," he said as he slid the second omelet onto his plate and sat next to her on the stools at the kitchen bar.

"Why do you look so different when you're working compared to your free time? It's not just how you dress, it's…everything," Sam said.

Fiona blinked at him, surprised that he noticed such a thing. "I do it on purpose. The things I have to see and do on my job…well… I would prefer to put on my work persona and have it something I can take off when

I get home. When the hair comes loose and the outfits change, I leave that world behind."

He studied her for a moment, and she felt her cheeks turn red under his attention. Fiona pulled her gaze from him and focused on taking a bite of the food. "This is actually really delicious."

When she returned her eyes to him, he had that teasing smile she was growing familiar with. "Don't sound so surprised."

Fiona rolled her eyes at him. "Well, it was my veggie-chopping skills that put it over the top."

He took a bite, making a show of savoring it. "Yes, definitely the exact right size of onion to make it perfect."

She laughed at that, and they fell into companionable silence while they ate their food. Afterward, she leaned back in her chair, stuffed.

"Ugh, I had better get going. I have to get up early for work tomorrow. This weekend went by too fast."

He winced. "Sorry that you spent it all on doing stuff for me."

She placed a hand on his shoulder to stop him. "As I've said, I want to help and I like being of use to people. I just don't want to put on my work hat again. It's going to be a long week."

Sympathy filled his gaze as he followed her to the door. "And I thought my job was difficult. Is there anything you like about your job? If it's this wearing on you, I don't see how you can keep at it forever."

Tears formed in the corners of her eyes as he hit on the question she had been asked by people for years. The question she had asked Nana when she came home looking a little worse for the wear. "There are difficult days, but if you look at the bigger picture, the end goal, of making sure kids grow up healthy and safe, it helps you get through."

The thought of all the families falling apart without someone there to support them and make sure kids had a safe place to lay their heads at night made Fiona's heart break all over again.

"How do you keep your focus on the good instead of all the bad you see?"

Fiona gave him a small smile. "My nana set up a small tradition that I continue to this day. I save every photo the kids draw for me, to remind me that it's all about them."

She thought about the binders full of artwork she had, along with the fresh ones she hung on her wall to come home to after work.

"I also save all the thank-you letters and happy family photos I get in the mail after closing a case," Fiona added.

Putting her first thank-you letter next to Nana's last had been a significant moment for Fiona. She only hoped that someday her stack could come close to the one that the woman before her had left.

Sam's smile matched her own. "Wow…that's kind of amazing."

Tears formed in her eyes—whether from happiness or sadness at missing her grandmother, Fiona didn't know. "I haven't told you the best part. My nana told me to keep a journal. And to only write down the good things that happened on the job each day, none of the bad. So when

I have a hard day, I'm supposed to go back and read it and remind myself why I do this."

All the lives her grandmother had touched. All the ones she was currently helping and would impact one day—it was overwhelming sometimes…but in a good way. But it was hard to do it all alone.

Sam surprised her by wiping a tear off her cheek before pulling her in for a hug.

He hadn't meant to draw Fiona into his arms. Their friendship was new and definitely not at the hugging phase yet, but she had looked so sad that Sam couldn't help himself. Fiona was the kindest person he had ever met, and the fact that she had to steel herself so tightly before going to her job every day…well, it was humbling. He saw a lot of hard things as a firefighter, but he got to leave the scene afterward and hand off the tough cases to people like her.

Sam wished there was something he could do to help ease her burden. The thought that she went home every night without someone to talk to and unwind with…it didn't sit right with him. He was thankful that she at least shared dinner with Gran every day, but if he knew Fiona, she probably didn't tell the older woman much that could potentially upset her.

Fiona was soft in his arms, and she didn't pull away. Instead, she pressed her face to his chest and started crying in earnest.

He melted, rubbing her back and whispering words of comfort to her until the sobs subsided.

She finally pulled back quickly, her face red. "I'm

so sorry I shouldn't have cried all over you. It's been so long since I just let it all out like that."

Sam stared down at her in concern. Her eyes were bright with tears and the skin underneath them was swollen. She looked...beautiful; the word passed through his mind. But still, he knew he should step away and put some space between them, but he was still holding her upright with his hands on her elbows. "It's all right. Obviously, you needed to. You are welcome to cry on my shirt whenever you want. I have more."

She barked out a laugh at that and wiped her face with her shirtsleeve. "I'll keep that in mind. I really need to go now, though."

He still didn't move out of the way, his body between her and the door. Sam's brow furrowed. "Are you sure you're okay to drive like this? You could crash on the couch if you like."

Fiona shook her head and called Sherlock to her, hooking his leash to his collar. "No, I have all my work stuff at home."

Finally, he stepped aside and opened the door for her. "Yes, I forgot that you have to put on your work Fiona costume."

She said her goodbyes and hurried out to her car. She was probably still embarrassed by her tears. Sam shook his head at the thought. She had been such a crutch for him during this rough time in his life, and he wanted to return the favor. If being her shoulder to cry on was what it took, then he would wear thicker shirts to soak up her tears.

His house felt suddenly lonely without her in it. Sam snorted at that thought. He had been so determined that living this single life without kids and someone to come home to was exactly what he wanted, but today had been one of the best days he'd had in a long time. He didn't know how he was going to give the girls back when it was time. Though judging from his brother's comments yesterday, it would be a while before that happened. He suddenly didn't mind, because seeing the girls smile filled him with a warmth he never experienced before.

And the longer he had the girls, the more of an excuse he had to spend time with Fiona. It was nice to have a friend outside his work at the station.

At the reminder of his job, Sam pulled out the list Fiona brought today with names of certified childcare providers who could supervise his nieces while he was at work.

The captain had texted today to check in and to say that Sam could take off all the time he needed. But since this situation was probably going to be more long-term, it was time to start coming up with a plan to integrate the girls into his regular life. They needed some routine, rather than just being in survival mode all the time.

He looked up several of the childcare places online and emailed the contacts at a few that looked promising. Hopefully, he would have something settled in a couple of days.

His phone rang and he raced to answer it when he saw that it was his mother calling. "Hey, Mom, how is he? Anything new happen?"

She was quick to reassure him that Ben was fine. "I was just calling to check in on you, honey. I know things have been hard the last couple of days. We're here with your brother, but it almost feels like we're doing the easy part."

He huffed at that. "Watching your son struggle to heal in a hospital bed is not the easy part. I'm eating chicken nuggets and taking the girls on hikes."

His mother let out a sigh of relief. "Oh, good. I'm glad you all are doing things that make you smile. I've been so worried."

While his world had been shaken in the past few days, and one usually wanted their mom in situations like this, he wished he could be the one there for her. "There has to be something else I can do to help."

She was quick to dismiss his protests. "We have everything we need. You taking care of my grandbabies since they lost their mama, and their dad is here…"

Her voice choked at that. "Mom…"

"I'm all right. It's just…my heart is broken, you know?"

He wanted to give her a hug, but instead just said reassuring things while she cried on the phone. When she finally calmed down, she apologized.

Sam chuckled. "No big deal. Funny enough, you're the second person who's cried while talking to me tonight."

His mother sighed. "I'm not sure the girls count. Babies and toddlers cry all the time."

"I wasn't talking about them," he blurted out and immediately felt remorse. Sam didn't feel right about spilling all of Fiona's problems to someone else. "I just had a friend over and she was sad."

His mother didn't pry further about Fiona's reason for her tears, but her curiosity went in a different direction.

"She? A woman friend? Who is it? Is it serious? Are you dating someone?"

Sam sighed, knowing he had set himself up for that one. "It was Fiona, the woman who has been helping me with the girls. Yes, she is my friend now, and no, there is nothing going on between us."

There was a moment of silence, and then, "But you want there to be?"

His mother's question set him on edge. If she were in front of him, Sam would be the recipient of one of her probing looks that made it impossible to lie. But thankfully, he could evade for the time being. "It's not like that."

She wouldn't let it go. "Maybe it could be."

"Mom…"

She interrupted him. "Just think about it. If not with her, someone. I don't like you being alone all the time."

"I'm not alone. I have my lovely nieces to keep me company now," he said.

Sam's mother huffed. "That doesn't count. You need another grown-up to talk to. Now more than ever."

He listened to her lecture him on the merits of dating for a few more minutes before she had to get off suddenly because a nurse came in to take Benjamin's vitals. Even in his injured state, his brother still had his back, Sam thought with a smile.

Still, as he lay in bed that night, his mind wandered to his mother's words. He had enjoyed his bachelor life thus far, but it was nice spending the evening with Fiona, talking and eating together. Had he been missing out on something more by just casually dating all this time and not having anything serious?

However, as much as he enjoyed the companionship with her this evening, he didn't dare let his feelings for Fiona grow to anything more... Did he?

Sam shook his head. No, he didn't want someone at home worrying about him while he was on the job. He would take fewer risks and that could cost someone their life. And Fiona had enough in her life to worry about without adding him to the mix.

Casual friends—that was all they could ever be. Resolute in his decision, Sam fell asleep trying not to think about how nice it was to hug Fiona tonight, or how beautiful she looked with her hair down.

Chapter Seven

Over the next several weeks they fell into a regular routine. Fiona would go over to Sam's house for dinner every night after work and help with bath and bedtime for the girls. They would usually sit and chat about their day for about an hour and then she would head home to prepare for the next day at work. She always remembered to bring some of the leftover casserole to Carol. Fiona felt a little guilty about abandoning her evening chats with her neighbor, but Carol waved away her apologies and said helping her grandson was more important.

Sam went back to work, too. He found a daycare center that took the girls on weekdays, and Fiona volunteered to watch them whenever he had a shift on the weekend. "I feel guilty that you spend all of your days off here," Sam told her one Saturday as he was headed out the door.

"We don't stick around here much. I'm going to take them to the park today. Tomorrow when you're off we'll go on a hike again," she said.

Sam grinned at that. "It's a date."

Fiona's heartbeat sped up at that, but she pushed the thrill at his words aside. She and Sam had formed a nice friendship over the past few weeks. And no matter how much time she enjoyed spending with him, she had seen that even the best relationships come to an end.

Her friendship with Sam took up a large chunk of her time, but she loved every minute that she spent with him and the girls. It was almost as if they were a little family unit, even if was just temporary. And he really didn't need her help anymore. He was adapting well to life with two toddlers.

But he never asked her to stop coming over, so she just continued. Fiona would enjoy having something to look forward to every evening for as long as she could.

The next day their hike was just as eventful as the last time. No one came out injured, but Hazel finally realized that she hadn't seen her parents in a long time.

"I go home tonight and see Mama. She probably misses me," Hazel blurted out when they stopped for snacks halfway up the trail.

The little girl had asked about her parents periodically in the past few weeks, and they had just explained that their uncle was taking care of them for now.

Sam said that he was still trying to get his brother to see the girls and that having the conversation about their mom was up to him.

"I don't want to leave it to him while he's hurting, but I also don't want to say the wrong thing."

Fiona warned him that they wouldn't be able to put Hazel off forever, and now that moment had come.

Sam looked up at her, panicked. Fiona, who had to

have similar conversations through the years with other children, stepped in on his behalf.

"Hazel...your mama does miss you a lot, but she's not home right now. She's in heaven," Fiona started.

Sam closed his eyes, as if warding off the emotions that were coming.

Hazel scrunched up her face in thought. "With God?"

Fiona brushed the little girl's hair off her forehead. "Yes, exactly that, honey. And God is enjoying spending time with her so much. But she looks down on you to check on you to make sure you're okay."

Hazel's bottom lip trembled. "But I want to see her, too."

Fiona pulled her into her lap and wrapped her arms around her. "I know, love. But you can't right now. And she would want you to be happy and safe."

She looked up at Fiona with wide, tear-filled eyes. "What about Daddy? Is he in heaven with Mommy, too?"

Sam crouched down so that he was on eye level with his niece. "No, your daddy is just in the hospital healing. We need to let him get plenty of rest so he gets better."

Hazel's brows furrowed. "Daddy's hurt?"

Sam nodded. "Yes, but the doctors are helping him get better. And while we wait, I'm going to take care of you. Is that okay?"

Hazel nodded reluctantly before she started to cry in earnest, throwing herself at Sam and wrapping her arms around his neck. "But I want my mama."

He rocked her and let her cry all over him. "I know, baby girl, I know."

Fiona watched him comfort his niece. She knew from

experience that he was good at cheering someone up when they cried. Hazel fell asleep after a while, and, when they got home from their hike, they tucked her into the toddler bed that was set up in the spare room.

"I decided since she was going to be here longer, she needed a real bed," Sam whispered when he caught her looking at the new piece of furniture.

She just smiled at him and reached out her hand to Sam, guiding him to the hallway. His entire body was tense. That conversation had put a strain on him, too.

"You going to be okay?"

He leaned against the wall of the hallway, his eyes vacant. "I don't know."

She squeezed his hand again, just now realizing that she was still holding it. "Sam…you did a good job handling that situation."

His gaze finally met hers. "Really? Because everything I said only made her cry even more."

Her heart softened. The drive to fix everything motivated him. But some problems couldn't be solved. "You won't be able to make this go away for her. All you can do is be there to support her as she goes through it. She's blessed to have such a loving uncle in her corner."

It was more than a lot of the kids she worked with had. Sometimes, they would call multiple family members to try to get someone to take the children in, but no one would step up to the plate.

Not only had Sam done so, but he went out of his way to try to make things better for the girls.

"You're doing an amazing job with the tools you've been given," she said.

Suddenly, she was engulfed in his arms as Sam

pulled her in for a hug. He had held her when she was having a meltdown. Fiona guessed it was her turn now. They stood there like that in the hallway for a long time.

When he finally pulled away slightly to look down at her, Sam's eyes were filled with such tenderness that it made her heart clench.

"Thank you for being my friend. I didn't know how much I needed you," he said, his voice a hoarse whisper.

She hadn't known how lonely she was until he and the girls had come into her life as well. Fiona gave him a small smile. "I'm the one who has been blessed by all of you."

His face was so close to hers, his eyes studying her. For a brief moment she wished he would lean down and kiss her. Where had that thought come from? They were friends, and that was it. She was already emotionally invested into this situation enough without adding romance to it.

She believed that all romantic relationships were doomed, and she now valued Sam so much that she never wanted to risk going down that road with him.

"I…had better go," she said, stepping away.

"Fi…"

He looked confused and his entire body exuded exhaustion, from the slump of his shoulders to the circles under his eyes. She felt even worse now for thinking about kissing him when he was so vulnerable. She really needed to get out of here. Go home to her empty house, take Sherlock on a walk and be reminded of her normal life. All of this was just a temporary fairy tale that she had wandered into.

"You get some sleep. You'll feel better about this

in the morning. Maybe call your parents and tell them what happened."

He nodded and walked her to the door. "I'm glad you were here when she asked that. You helped me get over my panic."

Fiona smiled reassuringly. "You would have done just fine. But I'm glad I was here, too. It's better when there is more than one person to bear that kind of load."

She thought about Benjamin and the burden he would have moving forward as a single parent, but thankfully, he had a supportive family to help.

When she got home that night Fiona resolved herself to cut back on all the time she spent with Sam and the girls. Sure, he could still use some help, but she was growing too attached.

She wasn't meant to be part of a family unit like that. To do the work she had to do, it was best that she remain focused on getting through each day. She needed to go to court to testify sometimes about the things she saw. She had to carry crying kids away from their parents sometimes. She had to hold the hands of little ones in the emergency room while doctors documented their abuse.

When so many others lived in broken worlds, it was hard for her to be grateful for happiness in her own life. Her work was what God called her to do, and it was of the utmost importance.

Going back to work while juggling care for the girls had been a difficult transition for Sam, but he was getting into the swing of things. After a few weeks the guys finally stopped teasing him about how different his life was. He couldn't go hang out and watch the football game with his buddies anymore, unless he got a babysitter. He wanted to limit the time his nieces spent outside his presence to only the daycare while he was working, however. They were already going through a lot and needed the stability of someone they loved in their lives.

Even though they had done their best to explain to her what happened, Hazel still asked for her mom and dad every day.

His parents, for their part, made a point to make sure she got a visit from Grammy or Pops every few days, and a video call every day.

"We've tried over and over to get Benjamin to see them, but he's so broken right now. Nothing is going to change his mind."

Sam grieved along with his brother for his loss and pain, but he couldn't help the anger that was building in him with each day that passed without him stepping up to be there for his daughters.

His parents promised to keep trying, but Sam didn't have hope that it would do much good. His brother needed to forgive himself before he could move on. Sam had told him that when he visited again, but Benjamin responded that there was no forgiveness for killing his wife. His grief had blinded him to the truth of what had happened, and blaming himself was his only respite.

As the days wore on Hannah became clingier than ever to Sam. He ended up holding the baby to his chest most nights until she fell asleep. The nights that Fiona was there were better, because she would talk softly to him in a way that soothed both him and the baby.

Things had changed between him and Fiona since that night they told Hazel the truth. She started coming over every other day, and she made a point to leave the moment the girls were both asleep.

"I knew this would happen," he said to his best friend and fellow firefighter, Nolan, one day when they were driving back from a call. "I almost kissed her and now things are weird between us."

Nolan frowned at him. "But don't you want to be more than just friends with her?"

He shook his head. "No, not at the expense of our friendship. You know that I don't do relationships."

Nolan rolled his eyes. "Yeah, but I never understood why."

Sam scowled at his friend. "You know why."

"I really don't."

When they pulled into the station and hopped down from the fire engine, he turned back to his friend. "Remember that call a year or so ago, when Sanderson fell through the second floor and landed under the debris and we almost didn't get him out?"

Nolan shuddered at the memory. "How could I forget?"

"Yeah, well, one thing that's seared into my brain is having to make that phone call to his wife about what happened, telling her to meet him at the hospital."

Nolan tilted his head at Sam, studying him. "Yeah, but Sanderson lived."

Sam sighed, sitting down on the bench in the locker room. "But it was close, and we could have made a completely different call. He almost died, and would have left behind a wife and kids."

Not to mention their friend Andrew who had died on the job a year or so back. His wife, Becca, still brought treats into the fire station.

"I don't think I could turn anyone into a widow like Becca is. It's almost like she can't move on with her life. She's still looking for him all the time, bringing in those treats, clinging to the memory of a husband that won't ever return. I could never do that to someone. It's almost cruel."

Nolan plopped down next to him and shrugged. "It's a risk we all take. Any of us could die, and lots of men have girlfriends or wives. I don't understand why it would be harder for you."

Sam eyed his friend, who had recently reconnected with and started dating a girl he had gone to high school with. "You don't feel bad that someone might have to make that call to Harper someday?"

Nolan shrugged. "She knows what I do and did when we started dating."

Sam frowned. "Do you think if you married her and had kids, you'd be more cautious on the job so that you make it home to them?"

Nolan leaned back and studied him. "We're all supposed to be cautious on the job. Aren't you already?"

Sam chuckled. "Well, I am known as the guy they send up the ladder into the dangerous fire first. Would I still be the same if I had someone I was coming home to?"

Just knowing he had Hazel and Hannah was enough of a worry now, and they were his nieces. It was becoming harder and harder to drag himself to work each day.

Nolan shook his head. "I'm not the one to talk you

through this, bud, because Harper and I just started dating and we're nowhere near the marriage talk yet. But there are so many guys here who have been through it. I believe they wouldn't trade their family for the world, and they are still able to do their jobs."

That might work for them, but Sam didn't know if he could be the same way. His doubts were proven correct when he received a phone call a few minutes later from the daycare that the girls were in.

"There's been a situation. We need you to come over right away," the woman on the other end of the line said.

Panic and dread filled Sam as he clutched the phone tighter. "What kind of situation? Is anyone hurt?"

He was already walking toward the door. "We'll explain when you get here. Please just come as soon as possible," the woman said before hanging up.

Just then, the bell rang that another call came in. Sam looked between the car keys in his hand and his peers, who were gearing up.

"Just go, man. We've got this," Nolan said.

Sam didn't need to be told twice as he ran out of the building, proving that he would choose his family over the job any day. But did that mean he wouldn't be able to be a firefighter because he couldn't focus with a family?

When he pulled into the daycare parking lot, there were a couple of police cars out front. Sam's heart started beating faster. What happened to Hannah and Hazel? Did they call all the parents and guardians or just him?

He raced inside and the director of the center's shoulders sagged at the sight of him. "We're so glad you could get here quickly. It's Hazel…"

He looked around for his little niece, but didn't see her anywhere. "Where is she? Is she hurt?"

The woman bit her lower lip. "Now, before I explain, I want to let you know that the police are here and they are doing everything they can."

He turned on the woman, wanting answers. "What happened to my niece?"

She led him to the waiting room at the front of the building and prompted him to sit down. He didn't want to waste any more time; he wanted answers.

"Hazel kept talking all morning about wanting to see her mom. We were going to talk to you about it when you picked her up today. But we didn't know how serious she was about it..."

The woman cut off and a younger teacher stepped forward, her eyes filled with tears. "We were outside playing on the playground and one of the kids skinned his knee and needed a bandage. I only took my eyes off of them for a second to grab the first-aid kit. When everyone lined up to go back inside, Hazel was gone."

Sam was on his feet again. "How could you not mention that she was missing on the call? We have to go find her!"

The center's director stood up, wringing her hands. "The police are out searching now. They think she managed to slip out between the bars in the gate. They wanted you here to answer questions about where she might go."

He started pacing the floor. "Go? She's three! Even if there is somewhere she wanted to be, she wouldn't know how to get there."

Hazel was a bright little girl, but was still too young

to know basic directions. He ran his fingers through his hair in frustration. "I'm going to go out and look." The women tried to stop him. "The police said…"

"I don't care. I need to find my niece. You have my number. Call my cell if they find anything. I'm going to look around the neighborhood."

He pulled out and dialed his parents to tell them what happened. His dad was already on the way out of the hospital to come help before he hung up the call. Sam's mom would stay with Benjamin.

He looked up and down the surrounding blocks, searching for Hazel. He didn't see even a tiny sign that she was nearby. This was all his fault. He should have picked a better daycare center for the girls. He should have stayed out of work longer and watched them himself. Or he should have tried to explain his sister-in-law's death better to Hazel so she wouldn't have felt the need to go find her mom.

Sam made his way back to the daycare center and sank down onto the steps. His niece was out there all by herself, lost and alone. He wasn't able to help her when she needed him most. He was a failure as a guardian.

Sam pulled out his phone and called the one person who was always able to make him feel better lately when things were at their worst.

"Fiona? I'm sorry to interrupt your workday but it's Hazel…she's missing."

Fiona didn't hesitate for a single moment before saying the words he needed to hear. "I'm on my way."

Chapter Eight

Fiona's boss never questioned when staff was in and out of the office, because they frequently had to follow up on visits or help a client. This was why she didn't hesitate to just up and leave when Sam called. The thought of Hazel missing sent a shudder of fear through her. She was so little, and anything could happen to her.

Fiona drove to the daycare center and found Sam waiting for her on the front steps. He stood immediately and rushed to her, pulling her into a hug with an iron grip. "Thank you for coming. I don't know what to do."

She rubbed his back in soothing circles. "It's all right. We'll find her."

Fiona guided him back to the steps and they sat down. Sam shoved his fingers through his hair in frustration. "They've been looking for her for an hour now and can't find her. I walked around the neighborhood, but nothing…"

He explained that Hazel had been talking about wanting to see her mom all morning. Her heart broke for the little girl. "Did they send someone to the house?"

He nodded. "Yeah, she wasn't there. It's not like she could make it that far anyway."

His voice choked on his words. Fiona squeezed his hand, and they sat in silence, pondering their next move. Fiona's gaze roamed the building tops of the neighborhood, begging God for any hint as to where she could have gone.

And He answered. Her eyes caught on something and she stood up immediately. "I think I know where we can look," Fiona said, pointing to a mural on the side of a tall building a few blocks away.

The building with a cross on the top of its tower.

"We told her that her mama was in heaven," Fiona said.

Sam sprang to his feet and started walking in the direction of the church. They rushed inside, finding it empty of people. Not unexpected for a weekday afternoon.

A priest approached them. "Welcome, is there anything I can do for you?"

Sam walked away from the priest, looking around in every nook and cranny of the church's large auditorium. The priest's eyes narrowed in on him, but he didn't say anything.

"We're looking for a three-year-old girl who wandered off from the daycare center a few blocks away. We were thinking she might have come here," Fiona explained.

The priest gasped. "No, we haven't seen her."

Fiona explained the situation and the priest nodded, watching Sam with sad eyes. "I can start the phone tree and get some of our congregation out here to help you search."

Fiona nodded and thanked the minister for his efforts and started walking up and down the aisle, looking in every pew. A flash of pink caught her eye, and she leaned down to see Hazel, sound asleep under a pew in the fourth row. She let out a cry of excitement, and called to Sam. "I found her!"

She leaned down and gently pulled the toddler out from under the seat and into her arms. "Hazel, honey, wake up."

The little girl's eyes blinked open. "Mama?"

Fiona shook her head. "No, honey, it's Fi. Are you all right?"

Sam caught up to them and pulled Hazel into his arms. "Baby girl, I was so scared for you."

Hazel wrapped her chubby little arms around his neck, and Fiona's throat constricted at the sight. "Unkie. Don't cry. I right here."

Sam laughed through the sob that was choking him. "I know, love. I just am so happy to see you."

Hazel leaned back and looked at him, her hands cupping his cheeks. "I happy to see you, too. I look for Mama, but she's not here. And then I got tired."

Sam gave Fiona a helpless look. They had to figure out a way to explain this to the little girl so this wouldn't happen again.

"Remember how we said your mama was in heaven? Well, that means we can't see her for a very long time. But she's spending time with God, and she's happy. And she wants you to make safe choices now that she's gone. Can you do that?"

Hazel looked at Fiona with wide eyes before nodding.

"Come on. We need to get back to the school and let the police know that we found her," Fiona said.

Sam scowled. "I'm not letting her stay at that school anymore. Hannah and Hazel will have to go somewhere else."

Fiona nodded. "Yes, I think that's a good idea. In fact, I'm going to file a report to launch an investigation into the center. I know they didn't do this on purpose, but at the very least, they need to tighten their security so this doesn't happen again with another child."

The police agreed with her assessment, thankful she saved them a call to CPS because they had been planning on doing that anyway. "I'll make sure it's handled," she explained, and they gathered Hannah and Hazel into Sam's car and drove them home.

Fiona put a call in to her boss to finally explain what had happened. "Do you think you can investigate the center, or are you too emotionally involved?" her boss asked.

"I think I can do it. The girls won't be going there anymore, so I will just be evaluating it for the sake of other children anyway."

Her boss was quiet for a moment. "What about the uncle? Is this kinship placement a safe one? Should the girls be placed in a foster home until their father can heal?"

Fiona felt a surge of anger run through her. She knew that Sierra was just doing her job and her brain automatically questioned situations like this, but Fiona felt fiercely protective of Sam and the girls.

"No, they are doing great. This is, in fact, one of the better kinship placements I've ever seen. Sure, there were some growing pains at first, but their uncle has stepped up to the plate and done an amazing job. I wish that all foster parents were like him."

A throat cleared and she looked up to see Sam standing there with Hannah in his arms and Hazel wrapped around his leg. He must have overheard her defending him, because he had a big grin on his face.

"I have to go, Sierra. I'll be back to the office soon," Fiona said.

Her boss was quiet for a moment before telling her to take the rest of the day off to help Sam. "Oh, and Fiona? You're our best case worker, so if you say that those kids are in the best place for them, then I believe you."

"I do," Fiona said.

"Then that's that. I'm glad they have you on their side, too. I'll see you tomorrow."

Fiona hung up the phone and helped Sam load up the car.

"Thanks for what you said back there. It means a lot that you think I can do this," Sam said.

Her lips quirked up. "I know you can do this. And I also know you well enough to guess you are beating yourself up for what happened today. It's not your fault."

He leaned against the car door. "I should have explained it better to her. Somehow."

Fiona shook her head. "Sam, you offered the best explanation you could. You're making sure the girls are fed, safe, have a roof over their heads and are providing a sense of security."

He opened his mouth to add more doubts, but he was cut off by another voice. "She's absolutely right, you know. This isn't your fault. We've all been put in a situation that has shaken our entire world. All we can do is our best and trust God to handle the rest. But it's time we shifted gears a bit, I think."

Fiona's gaze caught on the newcomer, and she knew immediately it was Sam's father. He was just an older version of him, with salt-and-pepper hair rather than the solid brown. And a few more wrinkles, but not many.

"What are you talking about, Dad?" Sam asked.

"Pops!"

Hazel let go of Sam's legs and leaped into the older man's arms. He chuckled and pulled her up before turning to Fiona.

"I'm Dave Tiernan, grandfather to this little escape artist, if you haven't guessed," the man said. He squeezed Hazel a little tighter, probably just as relieved as all of them that she was safe.

"It's nice to meet you, although I wish it was under better circumstances," Fiona said. The man gave her a small smile and turned to his son.

"This situation has gone on long enough. While you're doing a great job with the girls, they need their father. They need your brother."

Fiona couldn't help but agree. However, she knew that Benjamin had been resistant about seeing the girls.

"He made it very clear that it wasn't what he wanted," Sam said with a sigh.

The older man looked between the two of them. "I think it's time we apply a little pressure."

Fiona didn't think this was a good idea. She was just a glorified babysitter in this whole situation, and a friend to Sam. There was no reason for her to be involved in any kind of intervention with a grieving father who couldn't bear to look at his children.

Yet, she somehow couldn't say no when Sam begged her to come to his parents' house with him for dinner before they all went to the hospital.

"You have to, or my mom will hunt you down. She's been after me every day this week to meet you," Sam said.

"I don't know why she'd want to meet me."

She had enough family dynamics that she encountered on her job; she didn't need to be involved in another conflict.

"Because Gran has been talking her ear off about you, and so has Hazel every time they've video chatted," Sam said. "You're one of her favorites."

Fiona couldn't keep the smile from forming on her face. "At least I'm up there with chicken nuggets."

They shared a laugh and Sam bumped shoulders with her. "You're one of my favorites, too. My mom is curious about who I've been spending so much time with."

Fiona's eyes widened at that. "She doesn't think that we're...dating or anything?"

She tried to keep the panic out of her voice, but didn't succeed.

Sam winced at her words, and she had to add, "Not that you're a horrible gargoyle, it's just... I don't date."

An expression of something flashed through his eyes, but it was gone before Fiona could make sense of it. Instead, he just winked at her.

"You know that, and I know that. And I don't date, either, but trying to convince Gran and Mom is a different story."

Fiona remembered Sam's explanation that he didn't date because of his job, but he was so good with the girls that it seemed impossible that he had discounted any possibility of having a family of his own someday. Still, it wasn't her place to pry. Maybe he would find the right person who would change his mind.

Carol's words about someone doing the same for her flashed through Fiona's mind. She studied Sam for a moment. If anyone were to shake away her notion that all families were doomed to fail, it would be someone like him.

But it wasn't meant to be because he had other priorities in life, too. It was funny that they had that in common, but it also kept them apart.

Not that there was any possibility of their being together. Even if Sam was the kindest, gentlest man she had ever met. Not to mention the way his eyes sparkled when he laughed at something Hazel had said, or the way he did everything in his power to help those he loved.

Where did those thoughts come from? She shook her head to clear them. There was too much going on for her to even consider that she and Sam were something more to each other than friends.

A feeling of panic filled her. She didn't want their friendship to go away because it got awkward between them if she, or he, pursued something more. Was the adage true that men and women couldn't be friends without wanting more?

Sam and the girls had become such a big part of her life that it would devastate her to lose them. That was why she had to focus on keeping things friendly between them.

"I just think that this is an activity that is for family only. There will be plenty of family around to help with the girls. You don't need me," Fiona protested when he started guiding her out the door.

"Come on, Fiona. It's just dinner. And if you don't want to go with us to the hospital to talk to Benjamin, that's totally fine. I get how that would make someone uncomfortable. But come eat with us."

She considered for a minute before finally giving in. But that didn't stop the nerves that filled her as she helped him load the girls into the car. "I don't know why it had to be tonight, though."

It felt like she needed time to emotionally prepare before meeting Sam's mother.

"We were all shaken by what happened this morning at the daycare, and my dad didn't want to waste another day. I agree."

Fiona glanced over at him when he slid into the driver's seat. He did look tired. The boyish joy she had seen in him when they first met at the station was gone, replaced with circles under his eyes and permanently slumped shoulders. "You probably want your life back," she said.

Sam shook his head as he pulled into traffic toward the hospital. "I will happily take care of the girls for as long as my brother needs. I just want him to see them. They are a family, and time together will help them heal."

Fiona closed her eyes and thought of all the families that hadn't been able to heal and ended up torn apart, beyond repair. It was heartening to see this family in the completely opposite situation—coming together to heal each other.

She was so thankful that the girls had so much family that was so willing to care for them until their father was on his feet, both physically and emotionally, again.

"Still, it will probably be a relief to be able to chill on the couch and watch an action flick without worrying that the sound of explosions will wake the baby," Fiona teased.

He tapped his fingers on the steering wheel thoughtfully. "You know, I thought that I would be anxious for things to be normal like that again, but I'm really not. My apartment will seem too empty and quiet when the girls are gone."

She thought of the too-large house she shared with Sherlock. "I know what you mean."

He shrugged. "I still get plenty of action-movie time at the station when we are waiting for a call."

She raised a brow. "I can't schedule a meeting with you all, but you have time to sit around and watch movies?"

He chuckled. "We can't predict when a call is going to come in, but there is a lot of downtime in between. You should just come around and hang out at the station all day and fit a meeting in when you can."

Fiona scowled at him, which made him burst into laughter. "I have enough work on my plate without having to wait around for a spare hour from you guys."

Sam winked at her. "Think of it as a nice vacation. Still, I can't argue with you now that a little foreknowledge in the care and keeping of babies would have been a good thing. I wouldn't have been lost changing a diaper, then."

Fiona snorted. "You wouldn't have been so flippant when I tried to help."

Sam reached over and squeezed her hand. "I always appreciate your help, Fi," he said. "But it sure is fun to get you riled up sometimes."

She sputtered out her protests in halfhearted outrage while he chuckled. But she didn't have time to come up with a good response because they had arrived.

He pulled into the driveway of a ranch-style home. It was well cared for, with carefully cultivated landscaping and welcoming decorations that set her immediately at ease. The white picketed fence was a nice touch, too. The exterior of the home presented all the appearances that an average family lived here, but Fiona knew better than anyone that the appearance of a home had nothing to do with the makeup of a family. Some of the nicest houses were kept by the worst people.

She tried to expel the negativity from her mind as she helped unload the girls out of the car. Sam was a good man, and there was no reason for her to be intimidated or suspicious of his family. She needed to shake that work habit. "You're here!" The front door flew open and Sam's father and a woman she assumed was his mother rushed outside. Fiona thought the grandbabies would be the first focus of their greeting, so she was very surprised when she was wrapped in a tight embrace.

"Fiona Shay, I've been waiting so long to meet you. You have no idea how welcome you are here."

With the warmth radiating from the kind woman, Fiona couldn't help but feel that she was in exactly the right place.

Chapter Nine

Seeing the shell-shocked look on Fiona's face when his mother tackle-hugged her was worth the visit, regardless of the outcome of their plan to make Ben see the girls tonight. Fiona had become such an integral part of Sam's life lately, and seeing her interact with the other important woman to him…it made his senses ignite with a strange feeling he couldn't identify. He had first felt it when she was at his gran's house, but now that their friendship had grown, so did that feeling. It almost felt like…contentment.

He chalked up his overwhelming emotions to lack of sleep and the stress of their family emergency. It couldn't be anything more. They'd had a rough couple of weeks and he was looking for comfort and joy in everyday things.

"I'm starving. What did you cook?"

Fiona elbowed him in the side. "Your mom's probably been at the hospital all day. You can't expect her to cook."

She turned toward his mother. "I'm sorry. I didn't even think about it. We should have brought something."

She waved away Fiona's statement. "Oh, we've got enough to feed an army between what the church has brought by and from my stress cooking. I tend to take to the kitchen when I'm upset."

Her husband kissed her temple. "I try to tell her that she's supposed to be resting when she comes home from the hospital, but she never listens."

Sam's mom winked at his dad. "We've been married for thirty-four years. You'd think you were used to it by now."

Dad gave her side a tickle. "Yeah, well, that doesn't mean a man can't try."

Sam grinned at the affection between his parents. They were still so in love after all these years together. He was used to their playfulness, but Fiona was looking at them with a wistful expression. He wished he carried pennies in his pocket so he could give her one for her thoughts.

Fiona kept a lot of what was going on inside her close to her chest, but it only made him want to know her more. She was a constant mystery to him, and he wanted to understand what made such a genuinely kind and giving person tick.

"Come on in, love. You can call me Molly. I don't think you're ready for 'Mom' just yet," she said, pulling Fiona into the house while he and his dad followed, carrying the two little ones. Sam rolled his eyes at her blatant matchmaking but couldn't fight a grin at Fiona's panicked look. She may want to avoid families after all the tough ones she saw on the job, but she was in for a motherly experience now that she was in the grip of Molly Tiernan.

The smell of tomatoes and garlic filled the air as he entered the house, and Sam let out a groan of pleasure. "You made your spaghetti!"

Her pasta was a favorite among the guys at the station. They were always begging him to have his mom bring in a pot. He didn't mind asking because he loved it, too. And his mom certainly was thrilled to feed a bunch of firemen.

It had been a while, though, with everything going on, so he was looking forward to a heaping plateful. Hopefully, Fiona wouldn't judge him for devouring the food like a wild animal. It really was that good.

His mother handed him a napkin with a doting smile before he dove into his meal. Sam sneaked a peek at Fiona and she was just watching him with an amused expression. "You didn't dive into my soup like that," she teased.

"Oh, you cook?" His mom looked delighted by the idea.

Fiona winced. "Unfortunately, no. Carol has been trying to teach me, but I just can't seem to get anything right. She's my guinea pig every night, and the girls and Sam got to have a taste a few weeks back. It didn't go well."

"It can't have been that bad," his mom said before turning to Hazel. "Fi's food was yummy, wasn't it, sweet pea?"

His niece made a face before shaking her head. "No, Grammy, it was yuck."

The entire table burst into laughter, including Fiona. Sam admired that she didn't take the criticism of her cooking personally.

"I'm just glad that Carol has taken pity on me and is trying to help," she said.

Dad leaned back in his dining room chair. "My mother is a one-of-a-kind cook. I do appreciate that you go over and check on her every day. I call her, but I can't always make it over."

Sam tried to get to Gran's house for a visit at least once a week, but it made him feel better that there was someone close by who cared about her in case there was a crisis. "I wouldn't have survived this past couple of weeks without Fiona, either."

Mom's eyes sparked as she glanced between him and Fiona. "It seems you are becoming a part of the family already."

Fiona had just taken a bite of spaghetti so she could not object, but a full mouth did not stop Hazel from weighing in. "She my auntie!"

All eyes went to the little girl. Her mother was an only child, and Sam wasn't married, so she didn't really have any aunts. "Where did you learn about aunts, sweetheart?"

Hazel picked up a spaghetti noodle and played with it. "Parker at school has an auntie. She sees her when she goes to her unkie's house."

It dawned on Sam where she had gotten the idea about Fiona. "And you see Fiona at my house a lot."

The little girl nodded. "Fiona is at Unkie's house. She's my auntie."

Fiona reached out and wiped some spaghetti sauce from Hazel's face. "Sweetie, your uncle Sam and I are just friends. I'm not your auntie, but I'm your friend, too."

Tears formed in the little girl's eyes. "You don't want to be my auntie?"

Fiona kissed the little girl's head. "Oh, sweetie, of course I do… I mean I don't… I mean…anybody would be blessed to be your auntie. But they have to marry your uncle Sam first."

Hazel's countenance improved after that. She sat up and beamed at them. "You get married! Addison from school was a flower girl. I be one, too!"

Sam was caught between a groan of frustration and hiding his amusement as Fiona's face turned red. He didn't want his niece joining the ranks of matchmaking women in his family. However, it was hilarious to watch Fiona try to dig herself out of the hole she had just gotten herself into.

His mom saved the day, however. "I think you would make a lovely flower girl, but you need to be patient."

Hazel scowled. "Mama said I has no patientness."

Sam's heart clenched at the mention of his sister-in-law. His mom wiped a tear before answering the girl.

"It takes practice. But we can start working on patience while we wait for your uncle to ask someone to marry him. Will you practice with me?"

Hazel gave her grandmother a doubtful look, but finally shrugged. "Don't know why he won't ask Fi. She's right there. But I wait with you, Grammy."

Great, now he had three generations watching and waiting for him to tie the knot. Just what he needed, Sam thought.

"You're going to get a lot of practice in," he teased, and his mom gave him the stern look that she bestowed on him as a child when he was too wiggly in church.

"Samuel Tiernan, stop that. You're going to hurt Fiona's feelings," Mom said.

Fiona dropped her fork into her bowl; the clatter made everyone turn toward her. She sat there with wide eyes and her mouth open. "I'm not... I... What I mean is I'm sorry if we led you to believe otherwise, but Sam and I aren't romantically involved in any way."

His mother patted her hand. "So you said, love. But I've seen the way the two of you look at each other."

What was she talking about? He didn't look at Fiona any way other than as someone who had practically saved his life when it came to taking care of small children.

"That's enough, Mom. I'm happy as a bachelor. Just leave it," Sam said in a harsh voice.

Mom opened her mouth to argue, but Fiona got there first. "And while I do enjoy your son's company... I don't plan on marrying him, or anybody."

He knew that she felt that way about the institution, and he certainly wasn't interested in it, either, but it was still jarring to Sam every time she said it. Someone like Fiona deserved someone to love and cherish her.

"But why, dear?" his mother asked. "Don't you want to find someone to spend the rest of your life with?"

Fiona shook her head. "I've seen too many marriages and families fall apart. It's not for me."

His mother wouldn't let it go. "My husband and I have been together for decades. It's possible. You shouldn't give up hope."

Fiona shifted in her seat, not meeting his mother's eyes. He needed to change the subject to get the attention off her so she wasn't uncomfortable anymore.

"Don't you think we should be talking about our reason for getting together tonight? What are we going to do about Ben?"

Fiona shot him a look of gratitude before putting her napkin on the table. "Will you excuse me? I need to use the restroom."

His mother gave her directions and turned back to the conversation at hand, arguing with Dad about whether or not Benjamin could handle "tough love" right now. Sam's focus was on Fiona, and how she was biting her lip as she left the room. Was she fighting tears? His mother was a busybody when it came to relationships, but he hoped she hadn't pressed Fiona too hard.

Sam wanted to go after her, but he was needed in this conversation, too. "I agree with Dad. He needs some sense talked into him. And we can't let another day go by without helping him."

His father gave a hard nod and finally Mom gave a sigh and leaned back in her chair. "Okay. Fine. How are we going to do this?"

Sam leaned forward. "I've been thinking about this a lot. And I have a plan."

Chapter Ten

Fiona heard the voices of intense conversations continuing at the table as she leaned against the bathroom door. She knew she should probably get back out there, but she needed a few minutes to gather herself. It was strange that she was so affected by Mrs. Tiernan's—Molly's—words. The woman probably didn't mean anything by it; she just wanted to see her son happy and was determined to find him someone to marry. Fiona loved hearing about the strength of their marriage, but it was a stark contrast to what things were like in her own parents' house when her parents were always working and never had time for each other or her. It was no wonder they fought all the time now that they were retired and had to actually spend time together.

While the Tiernan house was peppered with family photos of their sons through the years, family vacations and holidays, her family home was meticulously designed by an interior decorator and showed no evidence of actually being lived in.

From what she had seen, marriages fell apart and

kids weren't loved like they should be. Both her job and her own upbringing taught her that.

Yet, here was a family who seemed to defy that trend, and she admitted to herself begrudgingly that she *had* seen others as well. Was a long and stable marriage and a happy family really possible? It would seem so.

Fiona closed her eyes and let herself consider the possibility that it could happen for her someday. Not that Sherlock wasn't wonderful company, but what would it be like to come home to someone other than her dog? To share meals with someone and go on hikes together? To talk to a partner about her job and her worries?

You already kind of have that in your friendship with Sam, she thought.

But all of that was temporary and would be ending someday, wouldn't it? A wave of sadness flooded through her at the thought, but she pushed it away. The priority here was to get the girls the help that they needed and to reconnect them with their father.

And maybe she and Sam could still be friends after that…because hopefully, he appreciated her a little bit outside of just her support with his nieces.

But regardless of how things turned out between them, this entire experience had shown Fiona that she didn't want to be alone anymore.

And she wasn't going to let that happen to Benjamin. She would do whatever the family needed to make sure he and the girls healed from this trauma.

Fiona wiped a stray tear from her eyes and rejoined the family, who were now sitting in the living room. Sam gave her a quizzical look and she squeezed his hand as she sat down next to him to let him know that she was all right.

"Fiona, I'm glad you're back. I was wondering if you could sit with the girls in the waiting room while we talk to Ben," Molly said.

Fiona nodded. "I can do that. Anything else you need from me?"

Sam shifted in his seat next to her. "We'll bring them in after a few minutes, but we were hoping you could come in with them to help Hazel feel comfortable if things don't go well."

The preschooler would need a safe person who was unbiased toward Benjamin and on her side. "I can pull her out if it gets too intense."

Sam leaned back and put his arm over the top of the couch above her shoulders. Fiona glanced at him through the sides of her eyes, but his expression remained neutral as he focused on his father, who was telling them some of the key points they should say to Benjamin. Maybe it was a subconscious gesture and nothing more.

Game plan in hand, they cleaned the girls up from their dinner mess and loaded them into their car seats to go to the hospital. They needed to get this done as soon as possible, because they didn't want to get too close to Hazel and Hannah's bedtimes and have crabby babies on top of what they were facing.

"Are you all right?" Sam asked after he climbed into the driver's seat. They were following his parents to the hospital.

"Yeah, I'm sorry. I just got a little…"

His lips quirked up in the corners. "Overwhelmed by my mom practically planning our wedding?"

She gave a nervous chuckle. "No, it's not that. I mean, she does need to be reminded that we are just friends," Fiona said. Sam glanced sideways at her words before tightening his hands on the steering wheel and focusing on the road again.

"Yeah, no reminders will be enough for her. She's not going to let it go," Sam said. "I'm used to it, but I'm sorry if she made you uncomfortable."

Fiona thought of how kind and friendly Molly had been when she arrived.

"It was actually the opposite of that. I'm not used to entering homes that are so welcoming and filled with love."

Sam's jaw ticked. "Yeah, I imagine you probably are not welcome in many of the places you go for your job."

She cringed at the memory of all the doors that had been slammed in her face through the years. "Yeah, I'm not their favorite person. But even my own home growing up was nothing like yours."

He glanced at her. "What do you mean? Aren't your parents still together?"

Fiona leaned back in her seat, closing her eyes as she thought about the cold environment she grew up in.

"Oh, they're still together, but I don't know why they even got married in the first place. It seems more like a business transaction to them. I was just a product of their merger, not a kid to be loved and nurtured."

Sam's hand reached over and pulled hers out of her lap. The warmth of the gesture helped her push more words out. "I don't even think they like each other anymore. Seeing your parents, so happy after all these years and obviously loving their children… It just reminded me of how different my experience was."

Sam let out a grumbling sound in his throat, squeezing her fingers a little tighter. "I'm so sorry that your parents did that to you, Fi. No child should have to be raised in a home like that."

She shrugged. "They didn't beat me or starve me. Believe me—I know from experience that there are a lot worse situations that I could have been in."

He shook his head. "That doesn't take away the pain they caused you. And it sounds like they did starve you…for affection. You're one of the best people I've ever met, Fiona. And you deserve to have people in your life that appreciate that."

She wiped a tear that rolled down her face at his words. What was wrong with her today that she cried so often?

"Thank you. That means a lot," Fiona said.

His thumb stroked her hand gently and she let herself enjoy the calm silence of the car and the comfort he was providing. Hannah let out a snore in the backseat and they both chuckled.

"It's going to be hard to get them to go to bed tonight if they're sleeping in the car now," she said.

Sam rolled his eyes. "Story of my life."

They carried the sleeping girls out of the car seats and through the hospital to the waiting room on Benjamin's floor. Hazel perked up when they sat her down in a chair, asking if she could have a snack from the vending machine.

Fiona pulled some money out of her purse and smiled

at the Tiernan family. "I've got the sugar therapy handled. You guys go ahead."

Sam looked between the girls and the door to Benjamin's room. His legs shifted and he ran his fingers through his hair. She noticed he did that when he was stressed or at a loss for what to do next.

On a whim, she crossed to him and wrapped her arms around him in a hug. "It's going to be all right. You've got this. You love your brother and you're doing what's best for him and the girls."

Sam enveloped her into a hug of his own and kissed the top of Fiona's head. Warmth filled her as she let the comfort erase all the feelings she had been processing in the car on the way here.

Yeah, I'm not giving this friendship up for anything, Fiona thought as she finally stepped back.

"Come on, Hazelnut. Let's pick out a yummy treat," she said. With a final wave to the Tiernans, Fiona let the little girl pull her toward the food.

"I want gummies!"

Fiona laughed as the little girl pointed out something on each row of the display that she wanted. Thankfully, she wasn't upset that the vending machine did not carry chicken nuggets.

"How about you pick one thing and I do, too, and we can share?"

Hazel tilted her head in thought. "But I wants all the things."

Craving chocolate herself, Fiona certainly could understand, but she didn't want to send an exceedingly hyper child home with Sam that evening.

"Let's just stick with one for now and then if we're here too long, we can get another."

That seemed to pacify Hazel, and they each picked their treat and settled down in the waiting room.

She tried to keep the little girl occupied with a game of "I spy," but Hazel was wide-eyed at all the hospital activity that passed the waiting room. She was particularly interested in people being wheeled by in hospital beds.

"Lots of sick people here, Fi?"

Fiona nodded. "Yep, and the doctors and nurses are working hard to make them all better."

Hazel climbed up on her lap and looked at her with teary eyes. "Are they gonna fix my daddy, too?"

She hugged Hazel tight, praying that God would help them do just that, for the girls' sakes. "They are trying, honey. I hope he gets better soon."

"Me, too. I wanna see him. Maybe I can give him a snuggle and a mooch? That always helps me feel better," Hazel said.

Fiona felt a little wetness through her shirt and realized the toddler was crying. She rubbed slow circles on her back.

"What's a mooch?"

The question broke through some of the little girl's sadness because she leaned back and looked up at Fiona with a giggle. "You don't know about mooches? It's when someone you love gives you a wet, sloppy kiss on the cheek to make you laugh. You gotta do it loud, too."

Fiona bit her lip to keep from laughing. "Oh, I've never had a mooch before."

Hazel grabbed her face. "I'll show you, den."

She gave Fiona the most slobbery kiss she had ever received, and the two of them were laughing hysterically.

Their mood was interrupted by angry shouts coming from behind the doors to Ben's room. Hazel looked at her with wide, scared eyes.

"Daddy? Why is he so mad?"

Fiona had no idea how to answer that question, but she could only hope that Sam and his parents would be able to get through to the man behind the screams so he could someday soon get mooches from his little girl...

Benjamin was asking the nurse frantically for his parents when they opened the door.

He looked smaller than Sam had ever seen him before. His big brother's panicked expression settled when they all walked into the room. If it was true that moms made everything better when someone didn't feel well, Benjamin was surely an example of that right now.

"I woke up and you were gone," he said, his gaze settling on Mom with a frown.

"I'm sorry, love. We had a family dinner and I wanted to make your brother's favorite spaghetti," she said, crossing to the hospital bed and laying a kiss on Benjamin's forehead.

His brother's attention finally settled on Sam, almost as if he just realized he was there. "Hey."

One word; that was all he got, thought Sam.

"Hey, man, how are you feeling?"

Benjamin shrugged. "I'm alive, I guess. How are... things?"

Sam's jaw tightened. "If by *things*, you mean your daughters, they are missing you…and their mom."

His mom sighed. "Sam…we agreed to…"

She paused when her husband's hand dropped on her shoulder. "We agreed to tell him the truth tonight, and that is what Sam was doing. In fact, I would say that those girls are only in one piece because they have an uncle who loves them."

Sam stiffened with pride at his father's words. He knew that they had been counting on him to take care of Hazel and Hannah, but hearing his father speak up for him like that felt good.

"I don't want to talk about them," Benjamin said, turning away from them and looking out the window. He always seemed to do that when his daughters were brought up. It was one of the things they talked about this afternoon when coming up with a plan.

"Well, too bad. Because we're going to talk about it," his father said. They flanked the bed. Mom cut into Ben's line of sight between him and the window. Dad took the other side of the bed, and Sam stood at the end. Anywhere Ben turned, he would see a family member.

He couldn't hide from what they had to say. "Please, I just need rest."

Dad placed a hand on his shoulder. "And the girls need you."

Benjamin stared down the bed to Sam. "They don't. They have Sam. I trust him to care for them."

Under any other circumstances, the words would be reassuring, but he didn't need his brother's trust now. Sam needed him to be brave enough to heal.

"I will protect those girls with my life, but I'm not

their dad. It's time, Benjamin. I'm happy to care for them until you're out of the hospital, but you need to at least see them."

His brother closed his eyes against the onslaught of emotions. *Well, that's one way to avoid looking at us,* Sam thought.

"I can't. I'm not the parent they want."

His voice broke with a sob, and Mom leaned in and pulled her son close. "Oh, my sweet boy, I know that you miss Beth, but they are babies, and they want you, too. They miss their mama, and by avoiding them you're taking away their daddy, too."

Benjamin was sobbing now. "But what if I can't do it? I'm not strong enough to do this alone."

Dad gripped Benjamin's hand. "You are not alone. Look around you. We're all here to help. We've been here all along."

Benjamin opened his eyes and met each of their gazes. "The nurse told me the other day that God doesn't give us anything that we can't handle, but I don't think that's true. I can't handle Beth being gone. I can't raise my girls without her."

Calling them his girls was progress, Sam thought. His brother had to go through these feelings before he could get past them.

"You're right," Sam said. "You can't handle it."

Everyone gaped at him. This wasn't part of the plan—they were supposed to be encouraging. But they also had promised to be honest.

"What I mean is that statement is false. God gives us things we can't handle all the time, but that's when we can fully rely on Him to get us through it."

His parents nodded, encouraging him to keep going.

"I have no childcare experience at all. There was no way that I could handle taking care of Hannah and Hazel on my own," Sam said. "But I didn't have to. God gave me the help that I needed."

Fiona was a gift from the Lord these past few weeks; of that Sam was certain.

"But what if I don't deserve help? I was the one driving when the accident happened. It's my fault that Beth died," Benjamin cried.

His brother was still wallowing in the guilt he felt for the loss of his wife. The family patriarch leaned forward and gave him a glare. "It's not about you. It's about those girls who will lose everything if you don't step up to be the man I raised you to be."

Sam nodded in agreement to their father's words.

"Your daughters need you to help them understand what's happening. To let them know they still have you, even though they lost their mom," Sam said.

Ben grimaced. "I still don't understand what we're going to do. I don't know how to make it right for them."

Their father pulled up a chair next to the bed and folded his arms. That was the same position he took when Sam and Ben were in trouble as kids.

"You're going to have to figure it out. You all need to grieve together," his dad said. "Or things could get much worse."

Ben scowled at his father. "My wife is dead. I can't get out of bed! How could it get much worse?"

His shout exploded out of him, and it was the most energy they had seen from Ben since the accident.

"Hazel ran away from daycare. She was missing for hours," Sam said.

Their eyes locked. "What?" Ben shouted; then his voice dropped to a scared whisper. "Is she okay? Did she get hurt? Where did she go?"

Dad placed a hand on Ben's shoulder. "She's fine. The police were searching but it was Sam and his friend Fiona that found her."

Ben closed his eyes in relief. "Where was she?"

Their mom squeezed his hand, wiping a tear from her eyes with another. "She was at the church, looking for her mama because we told her that she was in heaven."

Ben closed his eyes at the statement. Sam wished there were something he could do to fix this all for his brother. But their dad was right; the only way to deal with the grief was to go through it.

His thoughts were interrupted by the sound of footsteps at the entrance.

"Daddy!" Hazel said as she rushed into the room and jumped onto Benjamin's bed. He made a sound when she must have hit one of his ribs, but he still pulled his daughter close.

"Hey, baby girl…"

Hazel wrapped her chubby arms around Benjamin's neck as she lay next to him. "I been missing you, Daddy."

Ben's fingers shook as he stroked the toddler's curls and his eyes started to moisten again. "I missed you, too, pumpkin."

The toddler gave a contented sigh as she snuggled her dad. "I miss Mama, too. Fi says she's in heaven. But I want her to come back."

Tears started flowing in earnest down Ben's face. "Me, too, honey. But we have to do our best to make her proud from down here. Will you help me?"

Hazel looked up and frowned at him. "Don't cry, Daddy. I will help make it better."

The little girl leaned forward and gave her father a sloppy kiss on his cheek. Ben laughed through his tears, and Sam's heart almost burst at the sound.

"Did you just give me mooches, baby girl?" Benjamin said, wiping the tears—and toddler slobber—off his face.

Hazel gave a solemn nod. "Mama says they are the best medicine. That and laughin'."

Ben smiled at his daughter. "Your mama was right. Will you come and visit me every day and help me remember to laugh?"

The little girl's eyes widened before she broke into a huge grin. "Yeah, and give you mooches."

"It's a deal."

Sam was watching the scene unfold when he felt a warm hand slide into his. "I'm sorry that she rushed in here. She heard her dad yelling and was off in this direction before I could grab her."

He would probably need to have a little chat with his niece about this habit of running off, but seeing her so happy in her father's arms, he decided that could wait for later. "It's all right. I think everything happened exactly as it should have."

Seeing the light in Benjamin's eyes as he listened to his daughter talk animatedly about all the things they had done together, Sam was filled with hope. When

Benjamin finally took little Hannah in his arms and was surrounded by both his daughters, he knew that everything would eventually be all right.

Chapter Eleven

The next couple of weeks passed quickly for Fiona. She was swamped at work, so she found herself staying later to close out cases or go on emergency visits. After experiencing the closeness of the Tiernan family, it became even harder for her to witness all these other families struggling. But things were different now. She felt a new sense of hope for the future, not only for herself, but also for the children in her care and their families.

"I'm sorry that I'm showing up just as the girls are going to bed," she told Sam one night.

She hadn't been able to help with much other than tucking them in each night.

"It's fine. I think I've got the hang of it," Sam said.

She bit her lip to keep from frowning. While it was great that Sam had come into his own as a caretaker, it meant that she wasn't really needed around anymore. Her helping at bedtime was only an excuse to come over and spend time with them all.

"Really, it's all right, Fi. I've been taking them to see

my brother every day anyway. It's good for all of them," he said.

He must have interpreted her upset to be guilt about staying late, not that she was spending less time with him.

Mentioning his brother was a reminder that some-time soon, the girls would go back to their home. While that was a good thing, it would also mean they would run out of excuses to see each other every day.

Visiting Sam and the girls was the happiest part of her day, and she looked forward to it immensely while dealing with the harshness of her job.

"How's he doing?" she asked, trying not to let her melancholy show.

"Better every day. The pastor has been by to visit him, too. He's trying to help Benjamin with the feel-ings of guilt he has."

Fiona nodded. "He needs to heal himself so he can help the girls heal."

Sam winked at her. "Yeah, a very wise and angry case worker told me once that even young babies are impacted by trauma and their caregivers are an impor-tant part of their emotional well-being."

Fiona grinned. "She sounds like a genius. Maybe next time you should listen to her instead of being a smart aleck."

Sam tilted his head, studying her. "You know, I've gotten used to listening to everything she says now."

Fiona's cheeks turned pink and she looked at the ground.

"Oh, I meant to tell you that I don't need you to watch the girls when I work this weekend."

Fiona looked up from the dinner dishes she was washing for him. "What? Hazel and I already had plans to go to the park."

She was looking forward to it, especially the ice cream they were going to grab on the way home.

Sam shrugged. "My parents are going to start staggering their time with Ben, only visiting one at a time, so they asked if they could have the girls for the weekend. They want to spoil them rotten, as grandparents do."

Fiona couldn't argue with that. Their son's recovery had given the Tiernans less time to spend with their granddaughters. It would be good for them to spend the weekend together.

She gave a chuckle. "I don't know what I'll do with myself. I haven't had a day off alone in a long time."

Sam frowned. "Well, it will be good for you, then. You've given up way too much of your own time for us. A day or two of rest is just what you need."

She wanted to protest that spending two days alone in her house sounded awful after she had gotten used to company, but she let it drop.

"Sherlock won't know what to do with himself," she said.

Or me, she thought.

"I guess I'll go for a hike on Saturday. I can go up one of the more difficult trails."

Sam took the dish she handed him and dried it before putting it away. "That sounds like a plan. I don't work until late Saturday night, so I'm planning on sleeping in for once that morning," he said.

Fiona snorted. "I'm guessing you'll still wake up early because now you're used to it."

He groaned. "I hope not. I need my beauty sleep."

She doubted the handsome fireman needed any such thing, but didn't tell him so. The last thing she needed was to give him something else to tease her about.

"Do you think you'll work late tomorrow night, too? I promised Hazel we could go out for nuggies."

Fiona held in a laugh that he was now calling them by Hazel's word for them instead of the actual one.

"Probably. We lost another case worker last week so some of us are taking on her cases," she explained.

Sam's lips tilted downward. "But I thought you already had a full caseload."

Fiona sighed. "Yeah, but now it's overflowing. And it's not like we can just ignore families that need help. There's just not enough of us to go around."

Sam grabbed her elbow and turned her toward him, studying her with a tender gaze that made her heart do an extra little beat. "They are wearing you too thin. I'm worried about you."

Fiona looked away. "I'll be fine. I always am."

He put a finger under her chin to turn her gaze back to him. "But who checks in on you to make sure that's true? That you really are okay?"

She pulled away from him and took a step back. "I don't need anyone to check up on me. I'm fine."

If that definition included getting less sleep than usual and forgetting to eat lunch most days, then yes, she was doing all right. But he didn't need to know any of that. Fiona had spent most of her life taking care of herself and others.

"I need to get home to feed Sherlock. He's probably kicking his bowl around the kitchen by now," she said.

"Fi…"

She waved away his interruption. "We're okay. I just had a long day, and you're right. I do need to get more rest."

He followed her to the door and watched her intently as she grabbed her purse and keys.

"We'll see you for bedtime stories tomorrow, though, right?"

If Saturday was going to be the start of her spending even less time with the girls and Sam, maybe it was time she started getting used to it now.

"We'll see. Depends on how my day goes."

And before he could say anything, she was out the door.

When she got back to her car, Fiona laid her head on the steering wheel.

"I made a complete fool of myself," she murmured to her empty vehicle.

Why was she acting so emotional over this? She and Sam were friends, and would probably still be once their time with the girls was over. It didn't mean they wouldn't see each other ever again.

But she had grown accustomed to seeing him every day. When she pulled into her driveway, she looked over to see Carol sitting on her porch. At least she would have more time to spend with her neighbor.

She crossed her lawn to give the older woman a hug.

"How are my grandson and those little babies doing?" Carol asked.

Fiona gave her a smile as she sat down on her porch

steps. "All tucked in for the night, which is where I'm heading once I feed the dog," she said.

Carol studied her for a moment. "You look tired."

Fiona snorted. She must really look bad. "You're the second person who has said that tonight. I'm fine, just overworked. I'm going to have some downtime this weekend."

Carol nodded in approval. "You and Sam going to take the girls somewhere fun, or just spend the day resting together?"

Fiona stood and stretched. "Actually, it's just going to be me. The girls are going to their grandparents'."

Carol didn't bother to hide her disappointment. "But you and Sam can spend time together, still. You don't need the girls to do that."

She hated upsetting her friend, but she had to be honest. "I've only been over there every day to help with the girls. If they aren't there, what's the point?"

Her friend narrowed her eyes, as if she was trying to see through Fiona's words into her mind. "Aren't you enjoying spending time with my grandson at all?"

She loved spending time with Sam. The problem was that he only wanted her around for the girls. But she couldn't lie to Carol.

"I enjoy his company, yes. But I think it's best that we start getting back to our normal lives as soon as possible. It's not like things will be the same once Ben is out of the hospital, and from what I hear, he's making vast improvements every day."

Carol nodded. "Yes, it seems he's really turned a corner, and not just physically. I was worried about that boy. Hazel turned out to be the key to unlocking the door he had shut himself behind."

Fiona leaned over and gave the older woman a kiss. "Yep, they should all be home together soon. Speaking of which, I need to head to my own house now. My bed is calling me."

Her friend ran her hand along her hair affectionately and said her goodbyes.

"You make sure you get lots of sleep tonight, and think about what I said about Sam."

Fiona tried not to roll her eyes at her friend. Still trying to matchmake, she thought.

Still, as she got home and watched as Sherlock devoured his dinner, her thoughts wandered to her conversations of the day.

Did her feelings for Sam expand to more than friendship? Did he possibly feel the same way?

She shook her head. No, he had shown no interest in spending time with her outside of caring for his nieces.

But Fiona had to admit to herself that she wished he would. Fiona froze at the thought. She liked Sam. Like really liked him, as more than a friend.

When that had happened, she had no idea, but she couldn't give in to those feelings. Her time with Sam would be over soon, and it was just as well, because she didn't believe that long-term relationships worked anyway. It was best to avoid them all together to prevent heartbreak.

She just needed to figure out a way to put a stop to her growing feelings for Sam. Fiona had a feeling that would be easier said than done.

Sam ran a mental list of all the items that he had packed for the girls, making sure he didn't miss anything they would need while at his parents' house.

"I'm sure there will be something I forgot," he murmured as he hoisted the diaper bag over his shoulder and picked Hannah up.

"You ready to go, Hazelnut?"

She beamed and grabbed her stuffed animal, excited to visit her grandparents. "Fi calls me that. I like it."

Sam ushered her out the door. "Me, too."

"I miss Fi," Hazel said as she stopped patiently at the top of the steps while he locked the apartment door.

"Me, too," he repeated.

Fiona was avoiding him, or at least he suspected she was. Since their conversation the other night about the girls being gone this weekend and her needing a break, she must have decided to go completely without them. She hadn't come by the past two nights to help with bedtime, citing work exhaustion.

While he couldn't blame her since he had seen the circles under her eyes from the extra load she was taking on at the office, he suspected it was something else keeping her away.

The loss of her presence created an ache in his chest that he couldn't seem to heal. Sam had gotten used to seeing her face every day, and now his world was a bit dimmer without it.

He buckled the girls into their car seats and drove to his parents', singing along to the kids album that played over the stereo. He chuckled to himself as he considered how much his life had changed.

His mom was there with open arms when they pulled into the driveway, ready to scoop Hazel up into a hug.

"My baby girl! I'm so excited to see you. We're going to have so much fun!"

Hazel hugged her grandmother back, but turned a

worried look to Sam. "But who is going to read with Unkie at bedtime while we're here? He will be all by hisself."

Mom looked up at him with sparkling eyes. "I'm pretty sure that your uncle will find something to do. Probably television, if I know my boy."

Hazel gave her a doubtful look and turned her head to Sam. "What about Fi? She needs someone to play with, too."

Sam crouched down so that he was on eye level with her. "Fiona is taking the day off. She'll probably go on a hike. Or something."

The little girl's eyes widened. "You need to go with her. What if she falls like I did and no one gives her a bandage?"

Sam sighed, but before he could answer, his mom chimed in. "She's right, you know. You should join Fiona on her hike."

Sam groaned as he rose back up to full height. "She hiked plenty before we came around."

She studied him with the narrowed eyes of a mother who never let anything slip by her. "I think it would be good for you to spend time with each other without the girls around."

Sam leaned against the porch rail. "You need to stop trying to push us together."

Mom grinned. "Who's pushing? I already know that you like her."

His brows furrowed. "What do you mean?"

She reached out and brushed hairs off his forehead. "My sweet boy, I've known you from the moment you took your first breath. I know when you're crushing on someone. It doesn't happen often, but when it does, you get a little swoony."

He chuckled, trying to cover up the panic that was building in his chest over the possibility that she may be right. "Swoony?"

Her lips quirked up. "You get a sparkle in your eyes every time you talk about her. And when she was with us a couple of weeks ago, your attention was glued to her every time she was in the room."

Had he been looking at Fiona a little longer than necessary? She was beautiful. And he smiled when thinking about her because she made the world a better place.

He paused in his steps as he followed his mother into the house.

She was right. He did have feelings for Fiona. She was the missing piece he didn't even know was there.

His mother's chuckle pulled him from his thoughts. "I see you finally figured it out."

Hazel wandered to the other room to go find her grandfather, and his mother sat down to bounce Hannah on her knee. Sam paced the living room, trying to process everything.

"Just because I like her…that doesn't mean there can be anything further than that. We have to stay friends."

Could he still treat her the same way now that he had figured out that he was infatuated with her? That was all it was, infatuation. He couldn't let it become anything more.

"You'll never know if you don't spend time with each other outside of just what you have with the girls," she hinted.

Sam chewed his lip. Maybe she had a point, but it

was a different one that his mother was probably trying to make. He should spend time with her alone, just
to see if they could remain friends despite the fact that
his feelings had grown. He didn't want to lose her. And
he couldn't offer her anything more.

Not with the job he had.

*But you've been working all week and weren't dis-
tracted from saving people when you had Fiona and
the girls waiting for you at home*, his inner voice reminded him.

But that was before, when it was all temporary in his
head. He could never have a permanent family and put
them through the fear for his safety every day.

There was also the fact that she might not even have
any other feelings toward him beyond friendship. His
sudden epiphany could make things really uncomfortable between them and he would lose her in his life.

Sam needed to approach things carefully. Maybe
he would put himself to the test. Gran had mentioned
on the phone that Fiona was planning on hiking this
weekend as he suggested. Sam didn't have to be at work
until tomorrow night, so maybe he would join her in
the morning.

So much for sleeping in, he thought. *I have somewhere to be.*

If he and Fiona could still spend time together alone
and he could put his feelings aside, then they could continue their friendship.

But if he couldn't be around her without confessing
his feelings and making things awkward between them,
then he ran the risk of losing her forever.

Chapter Twelve

It was a dark and drizzly day for a hike, but Fiona decided to go anyway. She laced up her boots and put Sherlock on his leash and hopped into her car. Carol was not on her porch this morning, but she knew that she had Saturday prayer group over the computer. It had taken Fiona hours to help her set up the video chat among the friends, but they had all picked it up quickly. Fiona loved how they all saw each other in church on Sundays, but still acted like they hadn't seen each other in years when they saw each other on the video call.

She wished that she had friends like that. It had taken her a while to get out of her shell once Nana died. But spending time with Sam and his nieces had helped a little bit. Not only was she friends with them, but Sam's mom made a point to regularly check in, and Fiona started having coffee and lunch with a few of the women at work when they got the chance.

"In our job, you have to take the moments of joy where you can get them," her boss Sierra told them.

"Besides, it's good to know who you're in the trenches with. No one else goes through what you do every day."

But the ladies found that it was easier to bond, and more relaxing, when they talked about anything other than work. Fiona smiled at the memory of them talking about another coworker's love life and how she had recently reconnected with her high school sweetheart.

She did not, however, like when the romantic inquiries turned in her direction. Fiona loathed being the center of attention, and she wasn't into dating, so she tried to steer the conversation away from herself. Fiona was surprised to learn just how many of her coworkers were married or dating. Didn't any of them get the same feelings of hopelessness in their job? She didn't want to bring it up because she felt like the odd one out.

Her arrival at the hiking trail parking lot pulled her from her thoughts. It was starting to sprinkle, but she had on her waterproof boots and the trails weren't as packed as usual. She pulled out her phone and took a selfie with Sherlock and posted it online, so her mother would know that she was all right.

They had been texting back and forth all week but hadn't been able to connect for a phone call. It was just as well. Fiona's life was the same as ever and her mother and father weren't getting along. A phone call would only serve as a reminder of that.

"Man, I'm in a depressing mood," she told Sherlock, who decided to help by peppering her face with kisses. A giggle slipped out of her and she gave the dog a scratch behind the ears. "You're right, buddy. Let's just get out there and enjoy God's creation. No more grumpy thoughts."

She started up the trail, waving at an older couple who was just coming off it, holding hands. They must have gotten out here extra early.

Fiona pulled her camera out of her pack and started taking pictures of some of the plants she found along the trail, along with the views. She had an album at home of some of her amateur photography.

Halfway up the trail, she stood on a boulder to get a good shot of the creek bed at the bottom of the cliff.

She cried out when her boots slipped on the wet rock and she started falling backward onto the trail. She was just about to reach up her arms to protect her head from hitting a rock when she bumped into something solid that definitely wasn't the ground.

"Whoa, easy there, I've got you," Sam said as he guided her gently into a standing position. Fiona caught her breath before turning to him.

"What are you doing here?" Her brain finally caught up to what had happened and was now registering surprise at seeing him on the trail.

The corners of his mouth turned up. "What, no thank you for saving you from certain death?"

Fiona rolled her eyes. "I was falling toward the trail. But thank you for saving me from all the bruises I would have gotten."

He grinned and helped her put on her backpack. "You're welcome."

She turned to face him again. "Why are you here? How did you find me?"

As she studied him, she noticed he was breathing a little heavy and his face was slightly red.

"I was going to try to go on your hike with you this

morning, but you weren't at the trail we went to before," he explained.

Fiona's brows furrowed. "I didn't go to that one because it's more kid friendly. I wanted to do a harder trail."

Sam bent over and took several deep breaths. "Don't I know it. After I saw the picture you posted with Sherlock, I drove over to this trailhead and rushed up to find you."

Fiona bit her lip to keep from laughing as every word was an effort for him. "You ran all the way up here to catch up? I'm halfway through the trail!"

He shrugged. "It was worth it, but I'll be feeling it tomorrow while on shift, for sure. I think I'll let Nolan handle all the ladder-climbing duties."

Fiona had a sneaking suspicion he would be perfectly fine tomorrow, since firefighters made it a point to keep in the best shape. "Why did you come all this way to find me? Is something wrong with the girls?"

He shook his head and nodded toward the rest of the trail. "No, I just thought it would be nice to join you today. Shall we?"

She studied him for a moment, wondering what was going on here. She needed to keep her distance from him to protect her heart, yet here he was. Still, the idea of spending the rest of the morning together was appealing, so she just nodded and started to go up the trail.

It took a few minutes for her to become less self-conscious and start taking pictures again. When they got to a big boulder about three quarters to the top of the trail, they stopped for a drink.

"Can I see the photos you've taken today?"

Hesitantly, she handed over her camera. No one saw the results of her hobby, but she trusted him not to make fun of her.

"Wow, these are amazing," he said as he flipped through the pictures on the camera's screen.

"Thanks, I'm going to frame some of them when I get around to redecorating Nana's house and making it my own."

He studied her. "When are you going to do that?"

She shrugged. "When I find the time. Most of my vacations are spent visiting my parents back east."

He nodded. "That's nice that you get to go see them. Do they ever come out here? I'm sure your mother would love to help you decorate. That's totally something my mom would do."

Fiona shook her head. "No, they haven't been back since Nana's funeral. I think she's just too busy to want to come."

They started hiking again and Sam was silent so she thought he had dropped the subject. "Have you ever asked her to come?"

She paused in her step. She had never actually invited her mom to come stay. Fiona just figured that since she was living in her childhood home, she had an open door to come visit.

"Maybe I need to."

Sam smiled at her. "My mom was big on telling us that we had to invite her over because she was never going to be that parent that showed up unannounced."

Fiona laughed at the idea of Molly barging in on her son and taking charge of his apartment. "I thought that would be something she liked to do."

He shook his head. "No way. She said that her mother used to show up announced. She says places should be lived in and you have the right to a quick, frantic clean before a guest comes over."

She was starting to like Molly more and more every day. "That sounds about right."

Her home did need to feel more like she lived in it, and not just Nana's old house. Maybe tomorrow she would start brainstorming decorating ideas.

When they got to the top of the trail, both of them were out of breath from the climb. "Close your eyes and turn around," Fiona said to him. "You have to take in this view properly."

He did as she asked and held out his hand. "I trust you not to let me fall off the cliff or trip and roll all the way down the trail."

Fiona turned him around and put her hands over his eyes so he couldn't peek. "You saved me, so I suppose I can return the favor. Okay, now open them."

Instead of looking at the view, Fiona studied Sam's face as his eyes brightened and his mouth dropped open at the sights below. The town seemed so small from this height, and the valley that it sat in spread far and wide until it reached the mountains on the other side. The drizzle created a layer of clouds below them, the mist giving the entire view a darker filter.

"I can't believe I didn't even know this was here."

Fiona smiled and leaned back against the rock wall. "You've lived here your whole life and haven't come up here?"

Sam leaned next to her, not taking his eyes off the

view. "Yeah, well, mountain climbing always seemed so daunting. I didn't realize they were just hiking trails."

Fiona's lips quirked up. "Yeah, well, there are bigger mountains, but these ones are definitely easier to climb."

Sam groaned as he rubbed his thighs. "Speak for yourself."

Fiona closed her eyes and took several deep breaths and soaked in the fresh mountain air. This was one of her favorite things to do, and it felt right to share it with Sam.

And being here, on top of the mountain, she suddenly felt very brave.

"Sam, you know how I don't believe in happily-ever-afters or dating?"

He turned to her; his eyes narrowed and his fingers brushed against hers. It was almost like he wanted to hold her hand, but was keeping himself back. "Yeah, you've said as much. Why?"

Fiona looked down at her feet, unable to meet his eyes. "Well, I'm starting to change my mind. And if I ever decided to go after my own happily-ever-after, I would want it to be with you."

He was silent for a moment and when she finally lifted her gaze to meet his, there was a gamut of emotions on his face. Pain, regret, sadness.

She wished she could take the words back, but it was too late. He opened his mouth to speak, and she braced herself for the rejection that was sure to come. Although she didn't know what she would do if he reciprocated her feelings.

He was just about to open his mouth to speak when the skies opened up and it began to pour.

* * *

Fiona screamed and laughed when they became drenched as the rain beat against them. "Come on, let's go!"

She grabbed his hand and started pulling him down the mountain. While instinct told him to run because of the rain, they had to take it slowly since they were on a rocky downward slope and one missed step could have serious consequences.

They couldn't talk over the roar of the rainfall, so Sam took the time to think about her words. He wasn't even sure how they made him feel.

On the one hand, he wanted to shout for joy that she felt the same way that he did about her. No one had made him feel as alive and happy as Fiona, and knowing that she cared about him in the same way meant everything to him.

Still, he felt a little nervous that she wasn't completely ready to chase her own happily-ever-after with him. She had spent time with his family and with him, and for her to still not be ready grated at him.

On the other hand, he really couldn't judge. Hadn't he come on this hike to prove to himself that he could be her friend even though he had feelings for her? That even though he believed in happily-ever-afters, they weren't for him because of the job he had?

They had gotten themselves into quite a mess of feelings.

They were almost to the bottom when Fiona's foot caught on a wet rock and she plunged forward. He was unable to catch her in time, and she landed on her knee and then her body toppled, and her chin caught on a rock.

There was a lot of blood, and Sam felt a moment of panic. But his training soon kicked in and he helped her off the ground and lifted her into his arms.

She protested his actions, but he ignored her and made his way gingerly down the rest of the trail.

"You'll be fine. I have a first-aid kit in my car."

She scowled at him. "I'm fine now. I can walk the rest of the way."

He smiled down at her, wanting to kiss the wrinkle that formed between her eyebrows when she was upset. "I know, but just consider this practice for my job. Besides, you're already hurt, and I don't want you distracted on the wet trail and falling again."

Sam had carried plenty of people to safety in his job, but there was something extra satisfying about helping Fiona. She had done so much to lift him up in the past months, and it felt good that this was something tangible he could do for her.

She wiped at the blood on her chin with her elbow and he watched as it pooled again. He didn't think she would need stitches, but it would definitely take a while for that one to heal.

Once they made it to the bottom, he sat her in the front seat of his car.

"You don't have to do this. I can just drive home and take care of myself."

"Fiona, why aren't you letting me help you?"

She still wouldn't meet his gaze. "I…after what I said up there, I feel weird and awkward, and I just want to go home and curl up in some cozy clothes with a cup of tea and pretend like today never happened."

Sam's jaw tightened. While her words had complicated things, he certainly didn't wish she had kept them inside. They had a lot to figure out between them, but he knew they could never go back to what they had been before.

And after a week of her avoiding him, he certainly didn't want to go back to that, either.

He pushed his racing thoughts aside to focus on the matter at hand, bandaging her up. "Let me do this, Fiona. Please."

Tears filled her gaze, and he wished he could make them go away. By not responding to her declaration, she was probably taking it as a rejection. Even if what she had said was a rejection in and of itself.

Fiona watched the rain trickling down the windshield as he patched up her knee and chin.

They sat in silence for a while, just listening to the patter outside. "I don't want to go out there to get to my car," she finally said with a chuckle.

"There's no rush. We can stay here for a while."

Fiona finally turned her eyes toward him, and he was surprised by the sadness he saw there. "I'm sorry…for what I said on the mountain. It wasn't fair."

Sam placed his hand over hers. "No, I get it. And just so you know…um, same."

She tilted her head to the side, trying to comprehend what he had said.

"What?"

He shifted in his seat. "I don't really do love and relationships, but if I did, I would want it to be with you."

As far as romantic declarations went, it wasn't flowery or all that joyful, but it was all he had.

And then, unable to stop himself, he leaned forward and placed a gentle kiss on her lips.

Chapter Thirteen

Fiona and Sam pulled back from each other quickly and both of them sat back in their seats, hair pressed into the headrest, staring straight ahead. Fiona's mind raced, trying to process the kiss.

"What… What just happened?" she asked when she finally could form words.

"A kiss."

She gave him a sideways glance. "Yeah, I know that, but what did it mean?"

He reached up and gripped the steering wheel. "You don't believe in happily-ever-afters. Do you date?"

She swung toward him. "Not really. I'm not a casual dater, either."

His shoulders lowered—in resignation or relief? She wished she could know what was running through his brain now.

"I don't really do the casual dating thing. Hence my embracing of the bachelor life."

Fiona waited for him to continue, but he didn't. "Why did you kiss me?"

He leaned his head back against the seat again and

closed his eyes. "Because I really wanted to. I've wanted to for a while."

Fiona searched her feelings and decided that it was the same for her. Sam hadn't been just a friend in her heart for a while now. But that didn't change anything. Or did it change everything? "But that brings us back to the main question—what does this mean?"

Sam opened his eyes and turned his head toward her. His lips turned down. "I don't think it can mean anything. You're only just getting ready to look for a relationship, and I...don't know if I can have one with my job. We could try to remain friends, but..."

It would be weird and awkward now. She shouldn't have opened her mouth at the top of the mountain. And he shouldn't have kissed her.

"Do you think you could change your mind about not wanting to fall in love and get married someday?"

She hated how her treacherous heart was begging him to do so.

"I don't know."

If someone had asked Fiona a month ago that question, it would be 100 percent no. But now that she met Sam...

Her phone buzzed in her pocket and when she pulled it out, she saw a text from her mother.

Call me as soon as you can.

Fiona clenched her teeth in annoyance. The last thing she wanted was another long conversation with her mother in which she complained about everything wrong with her dad.

It was a stark reminder that love and marriage weren't always what they were cracked up to be. "I guess I don't know, either," she finally answered Sam.

His grip on the steering wheel got a little tighter. "So what? We just pretend like today never happened? We go back to just seeing each other to tuck the girls in at bedtime every night and nothing more?"

She needed to completely remove herself from his orbit, like she had tried to do before. "I don't think I can do that."

He reached out and grabbed her hand. "Fiona, don't do that, please. I hated everything about this week. We can find a way to still be in each other's lives."

She needed to leave before the tears started flowing in earnest. Why was this so hard? This was why she shouldn't have let herself get attached at all.

"I should go," she said, reaching for the door handle.

Sam, however, wouldn't free her hand. "Fiona, please. We'll figure out a way to make this work. We'll either let go of our stubbornness about relationships or make it through this together and come out as friends. We shouldn't avoid each other. It isn't fair to either of us."

Fiona closed her eyes to keep the tears in, frustrated that she couldn't make him understand how difficult this would be. "It will be too hard."

He brushed a tear from her cheek and waited to say anything until she opened her eyes and met his. "You were the one who taught me that I could do hard things, Fi. Please don't shut me out. My world is a brighter place with you in it, even as a friend."

She shook her head, finally pulling her hand from

his. Her phone buzzed again, and she held it up. "I have to go. My mom keeps texting me."

She opened the door and rushed out toward her car. Sam stood up out of his side and yelled at her through the rain. "I'll see you soon, Fi. This isn't over for us."

It had to be, Fiona thought. It was all too much. She didn't acknowledge his words as she started her car and drove away. She had made a huge mess of everything.

When she pulled into her driveway, she cried in her front seat for a while. The rain finally died down when she went inside her house. Numbly, she made herself lunch and forced herself to eat.

She needed to get past the emotions of the morning and start getting on with her life without Sam in it. And eventually, that thought would be less painful.

She finally pulled her phone out of her purse and sighed when she saw a missed call from Sam.

"Let it go. You have to," she whispered to him, even though he would never hear.

Her mother had left a couple of other messages, so she decided to give her a call back instead of texting. Fiona said a few practice sentences to make sure her voice was strong enough not to reveal that she had been crying.

"Mom, I got your messages. Is everything okay?"

Her mother's tone was so cheerful on the other end, it immediately set her at ease. "I'm fine. I guess my frequent requests for calls might have been slightly stressful. I'm sorry."

Fiona accepted her apology, but still didn't know why her mother had texted her. They usually only chatted on Sundays. She was a day early.

"Did you need something, Mom?"

There was a throat clearing on the other end. "I have to need something if I want to call and check in with my daughter?"

Fiona snorted. "It's not like we chat often, Mom. I'm not trying to be mean. I'm just worried something is going on."

Her mother sighed. "No, your father is just out of town for a couple of weeks on a business trip and the house is so quiet."

Fiona paused in filling her teapot at those words. Her mother was lonely. Fiona never would have thought that was possible with her.

"I thought you would be glad to get a break from Dad."

Her mother was surprised by her statement. "What do you mean by that?"

Fiona started her pot of tea on the stove before sitting down. "You're always talking about the arguments you have with Dad and how annoying he is and always in your space and interrupting your activities. I thought you didn't like to be around him anymore."

Her mother laughed at the other end of the line. "Oh, sweetie. That's just me venting after years of marriage. Your father may annoy me, but that's because we're retired and spend every moment together. There is bound to be frustration."

Fiona frowned. What she was saying didn't line up to everything she had listened to over the years. "But…"

Her mother cleared her throat again. "Honey, I'm so sorry if it seems like all I've done is vent to you.

I shouldn't have. I just used to talk about it with my mom and…"

Fiona felt immediately guilty. Her mom had been missing Nana, and she hadn't even thought about it in a while. "Mom, I'm always here when you need someone to talk to."

Her mother's voice cracked. "But now you think that I don't love your father."

She thought about her life growing up, about the cold environment when it came to emotions.

"But you guys were always fighting. And didn't show affection much around me."

There was a pause as her mother considered her words. "We're lawyers. It's our job to fight and we're good at it. Even with each other. And we never wanted to show too much affection around you because we didn't want you to feel uncomfortable."

Fiona couldn't believe what she was hearing. "But you didn't hug me that often or show much enthusiasm about parenting at all."

There was a sniffle on the other end of the line. Was her mother crying? She never showed so much emotion on the phone. "I'm so sorry, sweetie. I guess I was just so focused on my work and stuck in my analytical brain that I neglected your emotional needs."

Fiona felt like she was just an item on her mother's to-do list sometimes. "I understand."

"No, it wasn't right that I treated you that way. Now I understand why you moved to the other side of the country to be with your nana. She was always better at showing how she felt than me. I was like my father in that way."

Fiona had never met her grandfather. He had died before she was born, but she had heard that he was a hardworking if not serious man. "My perfect opposite," Nana had said when talking about him.

"So you do love Daddy?"

Fiona cringed as her voice took on the tone of a small child. Sometimes talking to one's mother had that effect on a person.

"Of course I do! I can't believe you doubted that after we've been married all these years."

Fiona was quiet for a moment. "Well, I've seen a lot of married people in my job that were absolutely miserable."

Her mother groaned. "And I wasn't helping with the weekly phone calls, either. You poor thing."

Fiona got up to take her whistling teapot off the stove and pour some water in her mug. "It's okay. I just have a less naive view of the world and relationships now."

Her mother was quiet for a moment. Fiona filled the time by adding sugar to her tea.

"Sweetie…is this the reason you've never had someone special in your life before? You never talk to me about dating."

Fiona felt her lips turn up. "Mom, not everyone feels comfortable sharing the details of their love life with their mother."

She laughed, but then quieted. "But there hasn't been one, has there. A love life?"

And then Fiona did the last thing she expected—she burst into tears. And soon, the whole story of Sam and what had happened poured out of her.

For her part, her mother listened intently and didn't interrupt until she was done.

"Honey, you have such a big heart. Between your job and the help you gave your nana and now with your neighbor...you just pour out love on everyone."

Though the words were sweet, they didn't sound like a compliment. "Why do I sense a *but* coming on?"

Her mother chuckled. "But you've closed yourself down to letting others return that love. You need to let people take care of and care about you. I know that I didn't always do the best job of it while you were growing up and you learned to guard your heart, but you need to open it up. Stop shutting down the possibility of future happiness with someone who will love you the way you deserve to be loved."

Fiona wiped a tear from her face. "What if I don't know how?"

"I don't think anyone knows how. It's something you learn as you go," her mother said.

Fiona laid her head on the table, wishing she had this conversation before she made a mess of things with Sam.

Her mother spent a few more minutes on the phone, talking about some of the things she was doing with her time while her father was away.

This is probably the longest conversation we've ever had, Fiona thought. *Maybe I was just as guilty of shutting my mom out as she was of me.*

"Maybe I should get a pet. I saw the pictures of your dog online. Too large for me, but maybe something small, that could sit in my lap and also keep me company," her mother said.

There it was; the loneliness in her voice again. Fiona remembered what Sam had said earlier about inviting her mother out.

"Mom, did you want to come for a visit while Dad's away?"

Her mother paused in her long rant about dog breeds and gasped in surprise. "Really? You want me there?"

Fiona blinked in surprise. How had Sam been able to guess how much her mom wanted to come but she had no idea?

"Yeah, I mean, I still will be working, but we can spend my downtime together. Plus… I've been thinking about redecorating Nana's house to make it my own and I'm terrible at that kind of thing."

That seemed to be the exactly right thing to say because her mother squealed in excitement. Fiona had to hold the phone away from her ear.

"I would love to help you with that! Mom never wanted to update her house, and it really needs some upgrades. And you have a way more eclectic style than her. We can shop together!"

Fiona found herself smiling for the first time since leaving Sam this afternoon. It was strange yet refreshing to hear her mother so happy.

"That would be awesome. My friend Sam's mom and my neighbor Carol would probably love to help, too."

Her mom could use some more people in her life. If all went well, maybe she could come out for a visit whenever Fiona's dad had an extended business trip.

"That sounds lovely, dear. Now, tell me more about this Sam…"

Needing someone to talk to who wasn't related to the

man in question, she leaned back and told her mother about their first meeting and beyond. Her mother didn't chime in with advice—she had already said her piece earlier—but it was nice to have someone just sit and listen.

No matter what happened between her and Sam, and if their friendship was gone forever, she would at least have him to thank for this. She had a newfound connection with her mother that she would never have had without him.

But now if she could only find a way to figure out how to move forward with him after what happened today.

She may have wanted to cut herself off from him, but it seemed that Sam was so embedded in her heart and mind, that wasn't possible.

Chapter Fourteen

Sam stared at his phone, as if willing Fiona to call or message him back. He wondered if it was hopeless to even believe that she might.

He couldn't believe that he kissed her.

Not that it wasn't a lovely kiss, but it had turned her into a scared deer in headlights before she fled into the rainstorm. And now he was stuck without her even as a friend.

A restless nap in the afternoon before work had not made him feel better, and he was dragging when he walked through the door of the station.

"Why are you limping? Did one of the toddlers kick you in the leg?" Nolan teased when he entered the locker room to put his stuff away.

"Nah, the girls are with their grandparents. I went on a hike this morning and practically ran up a mountain. Hence the limp," Sam explained.

His best friend threw his head back and laughed. "The things we do for love. I once ran a marathon to impress a girl. We're going to have permanent ligament damage if we keep this up."

Sam gave his friend a good-natured slap on the back as they entered the conference room for their daily briefing. While they generally had downtime between calls so they could relax, there were still things to be done around the station that had to be assigned. Sam had a sneaking suspicion that he was on dishwashing duty this week since he hadn't done it in a while.

"Yeah, well, my hiking days are over, I think," Sam said as they sat down and waited for the rest of their crew.

"Why? You and case manager lady get in a fight?"

Nolan was the only person besides his family who knew about his friendship with Fiona. And just like his parents, his friend insisted that there was a potential romance brewing.

They weren't wrong. But that potential was now dead in the water.

"Yeah, we've decided that there can't be anything between us. Between the stress and danger of the job, and her distrust of relationships because of her work and her parents, we were kind of doomed from the start."

Nolan gave him a sympathetic look and opened his mouth to reply, but a throat clearing at the doorway had them looking up to see the captain standing there.

"The earlier shift hasn't gotten back from their last call yet, so the meeting is postponed. For now, you guys are on dinner duty," Cap said.

Sam decided that it was probably a pizza night, because he had to conserve his energy for work.

Nolan met his gaze and nodded. They were on the same page. "I'll go grab my phone," he said.

Sam went to follow him when the captain put a hand

on his shoulder. "Hold on a second, son. I overheard a bit of your conversation."

Sam wanted to groan. Not another lecture from his mentor about how he needed to build a family of his own. Cap brought it up from time to time, and after his mother and grandmother, he was probably the next person in line who wanted Sam to settle down.

"I know what you're going to say, Cap. And believe me, I've been giving a lot of thought to your argument that it isn't all bad to have someone to come home to."

His brows arched in surprise at that. "Oh, really? I thought I would be talking to a brick wall again."

Sam rolled his eyes. "I'm not that bad."

Cap chuckled. "Son, last time we had this conversation you were looking for escape routes. Who's the girl?"

Sam leaned against the doorway. "You know that social worker who keeps trying to teach us about the safe baby drop location procedures?"

Cap's mouth dropped open. "Miss Shay? She's a really good woman, but I never would have put the two of you together. She's very professional and you're... well, much better suited to a life of running into fires and climbing ladders."

Sam snorted. "Thanks a lot."

Cap put up his hands as an apology. "I just meant that she is more of the office type and you're more of the relaxed type."

Sam shook his head. "She's not at all like her work persona. I think she sort of puts that on like armor."

Cap's eyes lit in understanding. "It is a very hard job that she has to do."

Sam felt a churning of sympathy for Fiona in his gut. One of his favorite things about spending every evening with her prior to this past week was that he got to help her unwind and relax every night. Whether chatting over dinner, splashing water on each other after cleaning up Hazel's bath mess, or just watching mindless television. She needed someone in her life to help her disconnect from the horrors of her job.

And he wanted to be that person.

"Wow, you really have feelings for her," Cap said, studying Sam in a way that made him shift nervously.

"Yeah, I do. And I'm working on sorting out those feelings. Which is difficult since both of us have hangups that make it impossible for us to want a relationship."

Cap laughed. "Sometimes those who protest the most are the ones who fall the hardest. Do you know my wife insisted she couldn't stand firemen? Her dad was a cop and she bought in to the whole rivalry thing for too long."

Sam smiled, having a hard time imagining a time when Cap's wife wasn't head over heels in love with him, and vice versa.

"Suited me fine, because I wasn't ready to settle down, but I just couldn't bring myself to get out of her orbit. God knew we were what was best for each other."

He got what the captain was saying, but that didn't mean he was willing to put Fiona through the worry for him while he was out on the job. And he didn't know if he would be able to run into a burning building knowing that he wouldn't make it home to his wife and kids. Maybe he wasn't built like the others on his crew.

"All I'm saying is that you shouldn't be so closed-minded. You need to be willing to consider that it might be possible," Cap said.

Sam had considered it. He had kissed her, after all, but now she wasn't even answering his calls and wanted to cut herself out of his life because she didn't think they could be just friends or anything more than that, either.

The girls were thrilled to see him when he picked them up from his parents the next day, and for the rest of the week, he was so thankful to have the noise and bustle they brought to his apartment.

His brother was getting better every day, and it wouldn't be too long before they all went home together. Sam was unsettled by the idea that his life would go back to what it was before the accident. So much had changed since then. He felt like a different person. Maybe he was.

One week after no contact with Fiona, he was getting ready to go into work when he got a phone call from Mrs. Newsome, the woman who was babysitting the girls for him now.

"I'm so sorry. I can't come watch them today. My husband is home with the flu, and I have to take care of him, and I don't want to give it to the girls."

He was grateful she didn't want to spread germs, but he would have appreciated more notice. These things came on suddenly, though.

Sam called his mom to ask if they could watch the girls, but his brother had a big physical therapy session today and needed his parents by his side. They were going to work on some of the things he needed to get the hang of before he transitioned back to his home.

Sam glanced at the clock. He had only thirty minutes until work. Gran was out of the question. She loved Hannah and Hazel, but it was too hard on her to watch them for long periods of time.

His fingers hovered over Fiona's contact information, indecisive. He hated that he was only calling her because of an emergency, but she was the only other person he could think of. Still, calling her would be difficult after they hadn't talked in so long.

Sam took in a deep breath and hit Send on her number. She hadn't answered when he called last week, but maybe she would today. To his surprise, Fiona picked up on the first ring. "Sam! It's so good to hear from you."

He wanted to say that the ball had been in her court when it came to returning a call, but he needed her help so making her angry probably wouldn't be a good idea.

"I'm sorry. I know I shouldn't call after you made it clear last week that you didn't want to answer the phone when it was me, but I really need help and I didn't have anyone else I could reach out to."

There was a beat of silence on the other end of the line.

"I can't believe things are like this between us. I told you that you could always count on me for help, and then last week I made you too uncomfortable to ask."

His eyes bugged out at her words. "You didn't. It was me that messed up."

Fiona sighed. "Sam, we really need to talk. Now that things have settled for a bit, and we've had time to think."

He didn't want to hope that it meant she had changed

her mind about the whole avoidance thing. That would just lead to disappointment.

"We do really need to have that talk, but I'm in a pinch today. My babysitter is sick."

Fiona, as usual, volunteered to help right away. "I'm just leaving the office. I can stop by on my way home from work."

He looked at his watch; he was going to be late, but not by much since she didn't work far from here. "That would be perfect. Thanks so much."

"You never have to thank me. I've missed Hannah and Hazel so much."

And me, too? his internal voice asked, but he didn't say it out loud.

Fiona arrived three minutes later. They could have had an awkward greeting, but Hazel launched herself at Fiona, climbing her like a spider monkey.

"Fi! You come to play with me?"

Sam and Fiona laughed at her excitement. "Yes, I did, Hazelnut. We've got a lot of dolly tea parties to catch up on."

The little girl gave her a thoughtful expression. "Yeah, they are so thirsty. I'm gonna get it ready."

Sam grinned as she raced off to pull the plastic tea-cups he had gotten her out of her toy bin. "You have made her day. I've been informed all week that I don't do tea parties properly."

Fiona raised an eyebrow. "Did you raise your pinky when you drank?"

He smacked his forehead with his hand. "I knew I was forgetting something."

Her laugh filled the apartment, a joyous sound that made his heart beat a little faster. "Listen, Fi, I…"

He was interrupted by his phone ringing. It was Cap. "How far out are you?"

He grabbed his keys from the bowl by the door, judging from his boss's tone that this was serious. "I'm about five minutes out. Leaving now."

Cap made a murmur of approval. "Good. Hurry. There's a big warehouse fire in Langdon, and they've called in all the surrounding fire departments to help."

Langdon was a small town about thirty minutes from here. They didn't have a large department, so they had to call in reinforcements when things were bad. But the fact they were calling in multiple departments meant the fire had to be huge. "I'll be right there."

He hung up the phone and turned to Fiona, but she waved him toward the door. "I'm fine, go. We'll talk later."

He frowned, knowing he had to leave but hating the things unsaid between them. "It may be a while before this shift is done. Big fire two towns over."

A crinkle formed between her brows. "Will you be safe?"

Unable to resist, he dropped a quick kiss on her worried forehead before heading out the door. She didn't pull away from him or look angry at the affection, so he took that as a positive sign that everything wasn't completely ruined between them. "I will do my best. I have our conversation to look forward to, so I'll be extra careful."

He laughed at himself—he had been afraid of relationships because he thought he wouldn't take additional risks on the job, but here he wasn't in one and he was already promising to be more cautious.

Sam made it to the station just in time to grab his gear and hop on the fire engine as it was about to pull up. "Thanks for waiting for me."

Nolan gave him a grim look. "It's really bad, from what I've heard."

Sam sighed and he leaned back against his seat, gathering his strength on the way there. It was going to be a long evening, and probably an even longer night.

Chapter Fifteen

Fiona paced the floor of Sam's apartment, waiting for a call from him that he was back from the fire. He had texted on his way to the other town that he would let her know when it was over, but that had been hours ago. The girls were tucked in their beds, sound asleep and unaware of the turmoil she was going through. What if he was hurt? What if he didn't make it back to the girls? To her?

Fiona sat down and willed herself to calm down. If this was what life was like for the wives of firefighters, she could imagine why Sam was hesitant to settle down. Still, she hoped that having the girls to come home to would mean that he fought harder to get out of bad situations and have an even bigger drive to push his way to safety.

"I'll just watch TV," she said to the empty apartment.

That turned out to be a big mistake because when she flipped on the television, the news station automatically pulled up and the big story of the day was the very fire that Sam was trying to put out. The flames were huge and encompassing the building.

Her heart beat heavily in her chest at the sight of it engulfing almost everything around it. Was he inside there?

She watched in horror as the building crackled and firefighters started to control the fire.

The reporter's droll explanation of what was going on was suddenly interrupted by shouts in the background. "Get out!" a man was yelling. Fiona recognized the person who ran by as the captain of Sam's station. "It's unstable! Get out!"

The news camera zoomed in on the building as several firefighters flooded their way out the doors and windows, but some didn't make it in time when the worst possible scenario happened—the roof caved in.

Fiona didn't recognize the sound that came out of her, half gasp, half scream. She covered her mouth so she wouldn't wake the babies and hurried over to crouch in front of the television, as if by looking closer she would get more answers.

Was Sam inside? Was he safe? She thought about texting him, but even if he wasn't one of the trapped firefighters, he would have his hands full trying to get people out of the fire.

Fiona groaned in frustration when the footage cut away from the fire and to the anchor in the studio, who was looking serious. The live stream of the blaze was still in a tiny box on the corner of the screen as the anchor recapped everything that was happening.

Fiona's knees ached, but she didn't move from that spot for an hour, desperate to hear any sort of news about Sam and the others. Her phone rang and she rushed to answer it without looking at the number, hoping that it was him.

"Sam? Are you all right?"

A throat cleared. "Um, this is Jessica Richardson, Mike's wife? He's on the same crew as Sam."

Fiona's heart rate increased even faster than it already was pounding. "Have you heard anything? Are they all right?"

Jessica waited a beat before responding. "I don't know the details, but I've heard that some of the firefighters from the station are unaccounted for. I got your number from Sam's gran because I wanted to make sure the girls were taken care of until he could get back."

Fiona shook her head, trying to process this information. Was Sam one of the missing firefighters? She didn't know how long she could function without more information. "I've got the girls until he's able to come home. How do I get news?"

The woman on the other line must have heard the panic in her voice, because she was quick to offer a comforting gesture. "These things take time. I'll tell you what. Some of the wives and girlfriends are going to meet at my house in a bit to wait it out together. All the kids will be bunked together like a slumber party. Why don't you bring the babies on over and sit with us?"

Fiona considered her words. Her only alternative was sitting here and letting her anticipation and worry build. Alone with her thoughts, she would only stress out more. Still, she wasn't Sam's wife or girlfriend.

"I don't know."

The woman wouldn't take no for an answer. "We have snacks."

Fiona didn't know if she could eat anything but decided to give in to the need to be around other people who understood the worry she was going through.

"I'll be right there..." She bundled the girls up and packed their portable cribs into her car and drove over to the address Jessica had given her. The house was in a subdivision peppered with small ranch-style homes. Cars lined the street on both sides, evidence that there were plenty of loved ones gathered inside waiting on news about the fire.

Fiona could hear the din of voices on the other side of the door, but it swung open before she could even ring the doorbell. "Oh, I'm happy you found us. I'm Jessica. It's nice to finally put a face to the name," a tall redheaded woman said. Fiona wondered how much Jessica had heard about her in the past...and who was doing the talking.

"Um, thanks for inviting me."

Jessica eyed the baby in her arms and the toddler holding her hand. "Let's get you some help."

She turned into the house. "Girls, we've got gear!"

Several other women hurried outside and gathered the diaper bags and portable cribs out of the car. Fiona just looked on with surprise. "You ladies are proficient."

Jessica laughed. "It's not our first rodeo. Come on in and meet everyone."

The mood was somber yet welcoming in the house, and there was also an overwhelming spirit of support among the people gathered. Mostly women, but there were a few men here, too. Jessica pulled her around the room to make sure Fiona met as many as possible without interrupting any conversations that were too intense. She was the perfect hostess.

"I'm so glad you came. I didn't know that Sam was dating someone," a woman named Ashley said by way of introduction. "We almost fell out of our seat when Jessica said you were coming."

Fiona felt her cheeks go pink. "Oh, he's not my... I mean we're not..."

Jessica placed a hand on her shoulder. "Honey, please. I heard the panic in your voice when I called. Even if you two aren't an official item or anything, you care about him. And that makes you one of us."

She did care about Sam and was scared that he wouldn't make it out of this before they could work out whatever was happening between them.

"So you're with..." It would take her a long time to figure out who everyone was and which firefighter they were connected to.

"Ryan. He's my husband. We've been married fifteen years and have a set of preteen twins. They are playing video games in the den right now."

Fiona nodded, catching a glimpse of various groups of people gathered around the room, talking in hushed tones. Some were hugging each other while they cried. Four women on the couch were holding hands and praying together. A table in the dining room was piled high with various food items and drinks, almost as if everyone had grabbed something on their way out the door. She felt bad that she hadn't brought anything, but it was her first time, so hopefully they would forgive her.

As if there was going to be a next time, she thought.

She and Sam were just friends, and she was only there because of the girls. The thought felt untrue as it crossed her mind, but she was determined to guard her heart against any kind of hope that their situation was anything more than temporary.

"We're like a family," Jessica said. "Come on. Let's go and get the girls settled and back to sleep. We have a room for all the little ones."

It took a while to get Hazel to finally nod off again with the excitement of being in a new place, but Fiona was finally able to rejoin the group.

"I miss when my kids were that little," Ashley said, offering Fiona a bottle of water. "Now they are balls of sass ninety percent of the day who need constant reminders to wear deodorant."

The group of ladies she had joined gave a small laugh. "Don't worry, they get better," an older woman said. She reached out to Fiona to shake her hand.

"My name is Tamara. I'm the captain's wife. He's told me a lot about you…and Sam."

Fiona shifted nervously on her feet. What exactly had been said about her relationship with Sam? The older woman had kind eyes, however, and gave her a reassuring hug. Fiona didn't realize that the act of comfort was exactly what she needed. She relaxed into the older woman's arms, tears filling her eyes.

"It's going to be all right. And if it isn't, that will be all right too, eventually," she said.

Fiona pulled away and raised her eyebrows in question.

"She means that sometimes the news isn't always good, but we are strong women and God will help us get through anything." A quiet voice answered her question. Fiona turned to see a small woman join them, her arms hugging her own torso.

"This is Becca," Tamara said.

Fiona held out her hand. "Oh, and you're with…"

A hush fell over the group, and Becca gave her a small smile. "Andrew. I was with Andrew. But…he didn't make it back on a similar day last year."

Fiona's eyes flooded with tears at the story. "I'm so sorry for your loss. It must be hard for you to be here today. Too many memories."

Becca shook her head. "My sisters were here for me last year, and I'll be here for them."

Fiona felt an instant connection with this group of women, but she also wondered if she really belonged, since so many of them had been through this before.

"I'm so proud of what my husband does, but I really wish I could put him in like flame retardant-covered bubble wrap before he goes to work," Ashley said.

One of the things that stood out to Fiona was that so many of the married women here had been with their spouses for a long time, a sharp contrast to what she saw every day on her job. How did they navigate conflict without things escalating past the point of no return?

"Do you ever fight with your husbands?" she blurted out and everyone's attention snapped to Fiona.

The older women raised their eyebrows and she groaned at her outburst. "I'm sorry. That was totally unrelated to the current conversation. I was just thinking about something else."

Jessica gave her a sympathetic look and laid her hand on Fiona's arms. "You and Sam been fighting, honey?

It's hard when they go into situations like this when the last things you said to each other weren't the kindest."

Fiona bit her lip to keep in the sob at the thought of all the missed time she had with Sam this week because she had been avoiding him. What if those had been her last chances to see him and she had shut him out?

"Um, not a fight...and we're not together but..."

Tamara interjected. "But you want to be, and you left things unsettled."

Fiona wrapped her arms around herself and nodded. The other women gave groans of sadness.

"Oh, honey, it's going to be all right. He'll get through this and then you'll be able to say all the things you need to say to each other," Ashley said.

A sob cut from Becca, the woman who had lost her husband during this type of emergency call. "Believe me, even if it doesn't work out, you won't remember the bad stuff, only the good."

The other women embraced their friend while Jessica put her arm around Fiona. "Believe me, sweetie, your fight or whatever was going on between you two is the last thing on his mind right now. If he has a moment to think about those he cares about, it's about getting back to them, not about any conflict."

Fiona in her heart knew that they were right, but she wished more than anything that she and Sam had that chance to talk before he went to the fire.

Being around all these women who banded together because they loved their fireman husbands, who stuck together during adversity, it was starting to put cracks in the armor she had when it came to believing in long-term relationships.

"What did you mean by your question earlier about if we ever fought with our husbands?"

Tamara's question pulled her out of her thoughts. "Do you want to talk about the argument you and Sam had?"

Fiona bit her lip as she considered opening up to these older women. "We weren't in a fight, per se. I was just wondering because when I'm on the job I see so many people who can't seem to make it work. You all seem so devoted…and I just wonder how you stay so strong through all the marriage conflicts you might have. Do you not have any?"

There was a round of snorts and all-out laughter.

"Oh, we have conflicts all right. We have some doozies," Ashley said.

Jessica nodded. "Two days ago I made Mike sleep on the couch because I had to remind him five times to take out the trash and one of the kids toppled it over and there was a huge mess."

Fiona cringed at that. On her job, that would have led to raised voices and violence. But these women could laugh at their conflicts.

"So how did you work it out?"

What she really wanted to know was what the difference was between all these people who could work through problems in their homes when so many others couldn't.

"A lot of patience. A lot of communication," Ashley said. "On both our parts. I'm a hot mess sometimes, too."

Tamara chuckled. "Sometimes?"

Ashley threw a popcorn kernel at her. "Okay, a lot of the time. We all have things that we struggle with.

But part of loving someone and being with them is enjoying their best and forgiving their worst."

Jessica nodded. "It's right there in the vows. For better or worse."

Tamara squeezed Fiona again. "I know that it's hard for you to believe that it's possible when you're witness to so much pain every day, but not every marriage works like that. Those are the exceptions, not the rule. I think you should make a point to get out there and spend time on your days off with different people in the community."

Fiona's brows furrowed. It was true that she didn't spend much time socializing outside her job. Was it possible that the isolation had skewed her view of relationships and what a happy family could look like? But she knew that even outside her job, not all couples were stable.

"But relationships everywhere fall apart," she argued, thinking of some of the couples in her parents' circle who had seemed so happy when she was growing up that were no longer together now.

Tamara sighed. "Unfortunately, that's true. However, maybe if you are around more people from places other than work, it will help you see there is a different ratio of success and failures."

Fiona sat down on the nearby stool that was next to the kitchen counter, processing the older woman's words. Before she could think any further, however, everyone in the room froze when Tamara's phone rang. "It's my husband. I'll get an update."

All eyes were glued to the captain's wife, the unofficial leader of the families in the room. She nodded with her lips in a tight line. Obviously, the news wasn't great, but everyone had to be patient for the details. She hung up the phone and held up her hand to get everyone's attention. Not that she needed to, because all eyes were glued to her anyway.

"The fire is about seventy-five percent contained," she said. "The main focus now is caring for those injured when the roof collapsed."

Murmurs of relief went around the room. This was almost over. "Is everyone accounted for now?" Ashley asked.

Tamara took a deep breath and Fiona knew what she was about to say. There were still firefighters in danger.

"They still haven't found five of them," the woman said.

She listed off the first four names of missing men and Fiona's heart stopped when the older woman's gaze settled on her.

"And Sam. He was in the center of the building when the roof came down."

A sharp cry tore from Fiona's chest as she folded into herself and prayed harder than she ever had before.

Some of the other women grabbed her hands and joined her.

"God, please guide others to find Sam in the rubble. Help him get out of there safely."

Fiona hoped that wherever Sam was, that he knew that he was loved and did everything in his power to get back to those who cared about him.

Including Fiona.

Chapter Sixteen

Sam woke up to the sound of someone shouting his name. It was dark and hot, wherever he was.

He did a mental inventory of what had happened before he lost consciousness. They had been helping with the warehouse fire. They thought everyone was out of the building and all efforts could be turned to extinguishing the blaze, but then the day took a turn for the worse. One of the workers had gotten past the barricade to run inside and save the office cat who was hiding in a cabinet. Sam and Nolan had been the two who went in after him, and they had passed other firefighters who were the last on their way out of the building when they heard a loud crash above them. Sam had caught one last glimpse of Nolan before falling into darkness.

"Nolan?"

His best friend had been standing not five feet from him when the roof collapsed. "Nolan, are you there?"

The sound of a moan to his left put Sam on alert. "That you, buddy?"

Another moan. Obviously, Nolan was alive, but he was in worse shape than Sam.

He did a self-examination of his body to assess his own condition.

"My toes and fingers can wiggle. I can't move my legs, but it's because of a weight. There isn't a lot of pain, just pressure."

He was stuck under something, but not significantly injured. His back was wet, probably from the water from the sprinklers on the ground. He didn't feel any wounds that would indicate that it was blood. His head was pounding, probably from whatever blow had knocked him out. Thankfully, his vision wasn't blurry and there was no dizziness for now.

"I think I'm all right. Now I just have to try to get us out of here."

Sam pushed up with his arms and was able to get one free from the rubble he was under. He reached for the radio on his neck but couldn't get it to work. It had probably been damaged in the fall. A loud, repetitive banging sound nagged at his ears.

"Is somebody in here?"

He had heard voices when he woke up, so there stood a chance that recovery efforts were underway. There was a shout, and then the banging noise stopped.

"Sam?"

Relief filled him as he heard a familiar voice, but it sounded like it was coming from a distance.

"Cap! Is that you?"

There were several shouts of orders for others to quiet down so they could hear each other.

"Yeah, it's me, son. Are you all right?"

Sam tried to push himself up into a sitting position but winced in pain when he did so. He couldn't pinpoint the location. Maybe he wasn't completely undamaged after all.

"I don't really know. I'm stuck under rubble, though, and I can't get to Nolan. I think he's hurt badly."

He tried to scan the room in the direction that his friend's moans were coming from, but it was too dark to see anything clearly. Small beams of light came through some of the debris, but it wasn't enough to illuminate the room. He squinted his eyes to try to make out where Cap's voice was coming from, but there was a lot of dust in the air, probably from the fall. That combined with the lingering smoke made Sam cough.

"There is a lot of debris blocking the way to you. We're trying to dig through, but it will be a while. Do you know if anyone else is in there?" Cap said.

Sam leaned back and closed his eyes, trying to hear if anyone else was in the room. Nothing.

"How many are missing?"

"Five, counting you," Cap shouted back.

Sam clenched his teeth at the thought of his other crew members somewhere trapped, injured, or worse in this wreckage. He prayed fervently that they would all make it out of here.

"You hang tight, son. We're going to get you out of there. We'll make it through this barrier in probably an hour or two."

Panic flooded through Sam at the thought of being trapped down here in the dark for that long. Did they have enough air? Did Nolan have that kind of time without seeking medical attention?

"What about the fire?" he asked.

Cap assured him that it had been put out a while ago, and Sam wondered again how long he had been unconscious. The roof caving in must have kept the area he was in barricaded from the blaze, so that was one thing he could be thankful for.

The sound of banging and power tools started up again. As Sam lay there and listened to the men work, his exhaustion seeped in, and his eyes started to drift closed. He was so tired, and his head was aching. Maybe if he just fell asleep, he could wake up when they were here to rescue him.

A voice in the back of his head screamed that it was a bad idea. If he had a concussion, it was important to avoid sleep. All the injuries he had treated through the years had taught him that it was essential to remain conscious. The way they always did that with a patient was to keep them talking and peppering them with questions so they had to stay alert.

But who could he talk to? Nolan still wasn't responding.

"Are You there, God? It's me, Sam," he said with a chuckle. "I know that You are, but I just needed someone and You're all I've got right now."

His eyes started to drift closed again, but he forced them open. "Please help me stay awake."

Why? He should tell God why he needed to get out of here without permanent head damage.

"The girls. I know I'm not their father, but even when they go back home, I'm part of their lives more than ever now. I don't want them to lose me."

Thinking of Hannah and Hazel brought a smile to

his face. That was it; he needed to keep talking and focusing on reasons to get out of here.

"Truth is I always thought I would never want kids. But if mine were ever to turn out a little like those girls, it might be worth it."

He imagined daughters with wild curls that their mama tried to put in neat ponytails and braids just like she put her hair in buns for work. He could picture them and their mother perfectly.

Sam blinked. *Fiona.* In his imaginary family, Fiona was the mother of his daughters. He started moving his arms a little more, as if the very thought of her spurred him into the action of breaking free.

"And Fiona, Lord. Thank You for bringing her into my life. I'm sorry I didn't appreciate that gift until I'm here literally trying to stay awake and not die."

He thought about Fiona, back at his apartment with the girls. He wanted more than anything to be there with her right now instead of here. The three of them had formed sort of a temporary family, but…

Sam gasped as he realized that he wanted it to be real. He wanted the whole wife and kids thing. He wanted it to be with Fiona. He loved her.

"Okay, God, I got the message, now. You've gotta help me get out of here," he said as he mustered all his strength and managed to pull enough rubble off his chest to get in an upright position. He groaned with the effort, but after checking himself out the best he could, there were still no serious injuries on at least his upper torso. He would be black-and-blue tomorrow, for sure, but nothing too major. As his eyes somewhat adjusted to the darkness, he could sense something above him.

He reached up to feel a beam from the ceiling a few feet above his head. It must have caught on something, and then also prevented larger pieces of debris from falling on him.

"Thank You for that one, God. This could have been a whole lot worse."

He closed his eyes, thinking of his parents, his brother, nieces, Gran and Fiona all getting the news that he had been seriously hurt. No, he didn't want to put them through that pain.

Sam decided he needed to get to his feet and find the others. That would help him stay awake. As he stood, a wave of dizziness flashed through his aching head, but he pressed forward, searching the room for his friends. He was able to find all the other firefighters from his crew, including Nolan. His friends were alive, although some were in serious condition and would need to be treated immediately.

Sam sat down in a heap on the ground next to his best friend. His head was starting to swim with dizziness. He had probably pushed himself too hard with his head injury, but he needed to keep moving and stay awake. Besides, he was better off than everyone else and he couldn't just sit still and wait for help to arrive.

He needed to rest his eyes. Sam leaned his head back and tried to focus on the sounds around him, but not letting them lull him back to sleep. He thought about his family and Fiona, and that he needed to stay awake so that he could see them again soon.

He was almost asleep when he saw a light shine in his face, and Cap was grabbing his arm.

"Sam, you with us?"

He nodded and tried to get up, but the older man put a palm to his chest. "Whoa there, son. Let's get the paramedics in here to help you."

He wanted to protest that the paramedics should take care of the others before him, but his tongue felt heavy, and he couldn't form words. His head injury was finally catching up to him.

Sam's eyes darted around the room, and he saw teams of EMTs working on the firemen who had fallen. Four of them. They had found the missing one.

They did indeed help the others first, while the captain talked to Sam in order to keep him awake. Sam's shoulders slumped in relief.

"I already called over to the house where all the spouses and girlfriends gathered when things got rough," Cap said.

Sam furrowed his brow. "What?"

The older man nodded. "Yeah, whenever we have a rough call, they get together and pray and support each other, especially if things don't turn out the way we want them to."

Sam thought about the day they had lost a firefighter, one of his good friends, a year ago. Had his wife Becca been surrounded by others to help bear the grief? "How come I didn't know about this?"

Cap snorted. "Well, you were the one who was being stubborn about not wanting someone serious. So you've never had someone on the phone tree until now."

Sam groaned as the EMT team finally made it over to him and poked his head injury. "It could be a concussion, but based on some of your other symptoms, they probably want to do a scan at the hospital to make sure there isn't anything more significant going on."

He didn't want to go near the hospital. Sam just wanted to get home to the girls and Fiona. But judging from the stern look Cap was giving him, with his arms folded across his chest, it wouldn't be an option.

"I let them know over at the house where everyone was gathered that you all would be headed to the hospital, so they will be headed over there to wait," Cap said.

But Sam didn't have anyone hanging out with the spouses and girlfriends. He had neither of those. The rush of sadness that washed over him was a reminder of how much he had shut the possibility of relationships out of his life.

"Why are you looking so glum, son? Your girls are going to be waiting for you when you get there," Cap said.

Sam's head shot up, the quick movement causing him to wince. "What?"

His boss laid a hand on his shoulder. "Fiona and your nieces were at the house with the other loved ones. And they are on their way to see you now."

Warmth filled Sam from head to toe at the thought of Fiona spending time with all the significant others of his firefighter peers. That was exactly as it should be. And for the first time since he became a firefighter, it felt like he had a family of his own to come back to after all.

Chapter Seventeen

"Look, it's Daddy," Hazel cried as she jumped out of her chair next to Fiona in the emergency room waiting area and ran to Benjamin's arms. He was being pushed in on a wheelchair by his parents.

"He's getting discharged today, so he insisted that we come down here and wait for his brother," Mr. Tiernan said.

Molly for her part looked like she was going to start crying at any moment. Fiona handed Hannah off to her grandfather before wrapping her arms around the woman. Sam's mother burst into sobs once they embraced.

"If I never have to see another hospital again, I will be a happy woman. Why do my sons insist on putting me through this?" Molly cried.

Benjamin snorted. "It's not like we're doing it on purpose, Mom."

Fiona pulled back and studied the man, surprised to see a more cheerful attitude in someone who had been at rock bottom a few weeks ago. There was still a hint of sadness in his eyes, which would probably be there for a long time as he mourned his wife, but he looked like he was actively trying to participate with his family again.

Judging by the way Hazel was clinging to him, the little girl finally had her daddy back. Molly gave Fiona's hand a squeeze before stepping back to scowl at her son. "Well, I'm getting tired of visiting my sons in the hospital."

Benjamin smiled at her. "I'm going home tonight, and Sam's hardheaded. He probably won't be in here for long."

The reminder of Sam's head injury took the levity out of their conversation.

"How is he?" Molly asked. "Have there been any updates?"

Fiona reached out to them on her way to the emergency room after the captain called to tell her Sam was being brought here and asked her to notify the rest of his family.

"They haven't let me see him yet. His captain came out to tell me that he's awake and talking, but they needed to get him a head scan and we can visit him when he returns from that," she explained.

Afraid that her fear for Sam would overwhelm her again, she busied herself with getting coffee for his family. Other firefighters and loved ones filled the waiting room, desperate for news on all the men who had been trapped today. Fiona was overwhelmed with the sense of comradery and unity within the group. This is truly what love was all about, not what she witnessed on her job every day.

The women she spoke with earlier had been right—

she needed to spend time outside work with more people so that she could be exposed to the healthy families of the world.

"Is the family of Sam Tiernan here?" an exhausted-looking nurse asked from the entrance of the waiting area. She and Molly rushed over.

"That's us. We're his family. How is he?" Molly said, gripping her hand as she braced herself for news, and Fiona's stomach fluttered at being included as a Tiernan.

"He's going to be fine. He has a severe concussion that led to some pretty serious side effects, so we are going to keep him overnight for observation. We'll do another scan in the morning to make sure there isn't a brain bleed or more severe brain injury, but for now, things look good," the nurse explained. "He has a cut on his back that needed stitches and his legs are black-and-blue, but I'm going to say it's a miracle that he is otherwise unscathed considering the circumstances."

The entire group sagged in relief that at least one firefighter was going to make a quick recovery. Only one night in the hospital wasn't too bad. Fiona worried about the possibility of the brain bleed, though. "Is he in pain? Will he really be able to leave tomorrow?"

The nurse gave her a reassuring smile. "He's been given some medication for the pain so he's a little tired. And he's really grumpy. Keeps demanding to see his girl, whoever that is."

Everyone turned to look at Fiona, who started wringing her hands. "But I'm not his girl."

Molly nudged her forward. "I think that you are, honey. Unless you tell him that you're not. And I don't think you'll be doing that."

Fiona chewed on her lip. She had put the brakes on anything more between them because of her disbelief in happily-ever-afters. But after her worry about losing him today…she didn't even want to think about a world without him in it. They did need to talk.

"I think I should probably go. This isn't the best time for us to be working all this out. Emotions are high today," Fiona said, but she couldn't get her feet to move from the spot she was in. Could she leave the building without seeing him when that was all she prayed about doing today?

"He's asking for you. We can only send one person back at a time, and you're the one he wants to see," the nurse explained.

Molly gave her hand another squeeze. "Go on, love. We'll wait our turn and see him in a bit. He needs you."

Fiona turned to look at all of them and saw nothing but encouragement on their faces. Taking a deep breath, she nodded and followed the nurse down the corridor. In some of the examination areas, she saw firefighters were reuniting with their wives after the ordeal. The sight added some speed to her step as she rushed to get to Sam.

When she stopped just before the treatment bay they had pointed out to her, she took a deep breath, preparing for the worst. But when she turned around the curtain, Sam's face lit up with a big smile. "You're here!"

His head was wrapped in a bandage, and he had cuts and bruises along his arms, but other than that, he looked to be fine. All the worry and stress from the past few hours caught up with her, and Fiona let out a big sob, crumpling in the chair next to him.

Sam winced as he sat up. "Hey, it's going to be all right. I'm fine."

He tried to slide out of the bed to get to her, but she put a hand on his chest. "What are you doing? You're hurt! You need to stay put."

Sam shook his head. "I'm not going to just let you sit there and cry without doing something about it. I need to comfort you."

Fiona scowled at him, as his stubbornness pulled her out of her tears. "I should be the one comforting you."

He smirked. "You're right. Give me a hug."

She rolled her eyes at him. "If I sit next to you on the bed, do you promise to stay in it?"

Sam nodded, holding up his hand. "Scout's honor."

"Were you a scout?"

She fluffed his pillow as he eased back into lying down on the bed and she sat next to him on the edge.

"Are you kidding? I got to wear a cool uniform and tromp through the wilderness. Of course I was."

Fiona tried to imagine Sam as a small boy. Her lips turned up in the corners because she thought he probably wasn't that much different than the man in front of her.

The man who had almost died today.

"Are you sure you're all right?"

Sam threaded his fingers through hers and nodded. "Yeah, I was just beat up by the building a little bit. The other guys have it worse. My head hurts, but I should be out of here tomorrow."

Though his words confirmed what the nurse had told her, tears threatened to spill out of Fiona's eyes again. "I thought that I would never see you again. When they said that you were one of the men that were missing after the roof collapsed…"

She cut off her words, closing her eyes to keep the memories at bay. Sam reached up and wiped away the single tear that escaped down her cheek. How could she have possibly thought she could go completely without seeing him? That they could only ever be friends?

Sam had become so important in her life, giving her someone to look forward to seeing after work. He made her want to do more with her life other than spend hours at the office and sleep.

"I'm so glad they invited you over with the others. I hate to think of you sitting alone with the girls at my apartment, worrying," Sam said, pulling her from her thoughts.

She shifted her position on the bed, not meeting his gaze. "Is it…weird for you…that I went to be with the spouses and girlfriends gathering?"

Sam leveled her with such a look of tenderness that it made her belly do a little swoop. "Not at all. I think it's exactly where you should have been."

Her heart raced at his words. She didn't think he ever wanted more out of a relationship—had he changed his views on marriage and family? She certainly had.

Fiona bit back a smile when she realized she was sitting there wondering what he was thinking and hadn't shared her thoughts yet, either. Honesty went two ways, and someone had to be the first to speak up. *It should probably be the one of us without the head injury*, she thought.

"I'm glad I went there, too, with all of them. It was

good to see so many long-term relationships that weren't falling apart," Fiona said.

Sam arched an eyebrow. "And how did that make you feel?"

Unloading years of anxiety about relationships was exhausting, but Fiona had a sense of peace that she hadn't felt in a long time. "Like happily-ever-afters are possible. I just needed to see a few before I could finally believe it."

A slow grin spread across his face. "And now you do?"

She decided to tease him to return the favor from the first time they met. "If I met the right kind of guy."

Sam's eyes narrowed. "And what would the right type of guy be?"

Fiona pulled her hand away from his and leaned back a little, folding her arms on her chest. She tapped her fingers on her chin thoughtfully. "Hmmm…he has to be a good man who loves God, is kind and is very good with children."

"Check, check and check," he said. "What else?"

Fiona tapped her finger on her lips. "I do really admire a man in a courageous profession."

Sam nodded. "Got that one down, too. I did almost die today and courageously pushed myself to get out and help my fellow firefighters."

The playfulness dropped from Fiona's mood at the reminder of why exactly they were in the hospital. "Oh, it doesn't matter what I think about happily-ever-afters. Because you don't want one, either. Because of your job."

Sam sat up and lifted her chin until their eyes met. "Maybe I had a change of heart, too."

Fiona's stomach fluttered at his words and at the sincerity in his eyes.

Sam watched a cascade of emotions play over Fiona's face. He had wanted to wait until later to have this conversation, but his near-death experience today had told him to seize every moment because he never knew what would come next.

"Fiona, this entire time I only wanted to be a bachelor and do my job and be able to take risks that no one else would because I had no one to come home to," Sam said. That time in his life was only a few weeks ago, but it felt like a lifetime.

Sam kept Fiona's gaze locked with his. "But the truth is that when I was stuck alone in the dark and afraid, all I could think about was you."

He had been so alone in the dark, with nothing more than his prayers. Having Fiona to think about made a significant impact on his survival. "I could imagine coming home to you every night, tucking our kids in, just like we did with the girls. Eating dinner together. Sharing stories on the couch when the house is quiet over a cup of coffee. Going on hikes up the mountain, with you bringing your first-aid kit every time because someone is bound to get injured."

Fiona let out a sound that was half laugh, half sob. Sam wiped another tear from her cheek and kept going. "I thought about our first kiss in the car. All this was what kept me going there in the dark when I was trapped. I got out of that situation for you. Because of you. Loving you didn't stop me from doing my job. It made me do my job better. I worked harder to save others and to get out of there because I knew you were waiting for me."

He had been wrong for so many years. He only hoped he hadn't come to the realization too late.

"I was so stupid to push you away. I love you and I want to have a life with you," Sam said.

Fiona's mouth dropped at that. "But I'm the one that pushed you away, after our kiss."

He chuckled. "There was mutual pushing. We were both scared because all the things we thought about relationships were getting thrown out the window into that rainstorm."

Fiona nodded. "I love you, too, you know. That was quite a speech."

His chest filled at the words. Even though she'd said them earlier, he didn't think he would ever get used to it. "I'm so glad that you believe in happily-ever-afters now because I want mine to be with you," Sam said. He pulled in a breath and steadied himself for what he had to say next. "Will you marry me and build a family with me? We already had enough practice. I think we're ready to go pro."

Fiona swiped her sleeve over her face in an attempt to stop her tears as Sam waited with bated breath for her to answer his proposal. However, she just sat there crying, so he decided to continue to convince her. He'd never proposed before, and maybe the hospital wasn't the most romantic setting. Sam had just blurted it out, totally unprepared. She deserved so much more.

"I don't have a ring for now. I'll go out and get one

as soon as I'm cleared to leave the hospital," Sam said. "I want to get it on your finger as quickly as possible, if you say yes, that is. I'm through with things being temporary when it comes to us."

Fiona cried even harder at his words. Sam's frustration grew as he waited for her answer. "I need to know what you're thinking, love. Are those happy tears or sad tears? How do I help you feel better?"

She frowned at him. "How am I supposed to stop crying when you keep saying things like that? I just get to the point of calming down and then you say something else so sweet that makes me cry again."

Sam couldn't stop the grin from slowly spreading on his face. "I'll try to keep my romantic declarations to myself until we can find a box of tissues, then," he said. "In the meantime, can you answer the question that I asked you?"

Fiona leaned forward and gave him a sweet kiss on his lips. "Yes, I will absolutely marry you. But only if you move into my nana's house with me once we're husband and wife. Sherlock hates apartment life."

Sam laughed, his heart light now that he had the answer he wanted. "I think that sounds like a great idea."

He closed his eyes and lay back against the pillow, saying a silent prayer of thanks. Fiona must have misinterpreted the move and leaned over his face, worried.

"Are you all right? Is your head hurting?" she asked.

"No, I'm fine. Just happy."

Fiona slipped her fingers through his and smiled. "Me, too."

He sighed. "I wish we could get married today. The girls are going home with Benjamin and my parents.

My apartment is going to feel so empty without everyone there."

Fiona arched an eyebrow. "How do you feel about a terrible slow cooker meal? I can invite you over to Carol's for dinner every night and you can try my new recipes."

Sam cringed when he thought about the tortilla soup he tried before, and she gave him a glare. "Don't even say anything. At least it's food and you get the benefit of time with me and your grandmother. And Sherlock."

He laughed, his heart lighter than it had ever been. "It doesn't matter what you put in your food, as long as I get to try it with you. Then it will be worth it," Sam said. "But maybe I should bring some pizza as a backup, just in case."

Fiona rolled her eyes, but her lips tilted up in the corners. "Fine, I agree to those terms."

And she sealed the deal with a kiss.

Epilogue

Two years later

Fiona laid her head back on the pillow and watched her husband walking around the hospital room, their new baby girl in his arms. He was singing a lullaby, one she remembered him singing to his nieces a few years ago.

"Are you going to hog that new baby all to yourself?" A voice came from the doorway.

Fiona turned to see Sam's parents pushing their way in to get to their grandchild, her mother not far behind. While Molly took the baby off Sam's hands, Fiona's mom crossed to her to brush her hair off her forehead. "How are you feeling, sweetie?"

Fiona smiled up at her mom. Their relationship had improved dramatically over the past few years after they started to spend more time together. Her father had even come to visit a few times. These past few weeks, she was surprised when her mother came to stay during the last days of her pregnancy, helping out by making meals and finishing the nursery.

And throwing her a surprise baby shower with her friends from work and the firefighter wives and girl-friends. Fiona couldn't believe that in a few short years, she had gone from being alone with only her dog and next-door neighbor as company to having all these people in her life.

"I'm perfect," Fiona finally answered her mother. "I got a little sleep and I feel much better."

Sam sat down next to her and threaded their hands together. "She's more than perfect. She's a rock star. I can't believe what women go through to bring children into this world."

Fiona arched a brow at that. "You've seen a few baby deliveries on the job."

He shrugged. "Yeah, but it's much more harrowing when it's someone you love going through all that pain. Seriously, love, you amaze me."

Fiona basked in the glow of his words. It was hard to imagine that she had ever doubted that they would be happily married. She couldn't imagine life without him. Sure, they had their moments where they didn't get along, but through patience, prayer and a little help from their friends and family sometimes, they got through them.

A nurse came in the door and announced that there were more people in the waiting room wanting to see the baby, so the grandparents needed to give someone else a turn.

"Fine, but we'll be back later," Molly said in a huff. "I'll entertain myself with the other grandkids that are probably waiting out there, too."

Fiona was thrilled with the idea of Hannah and Hazel

visiting, but Carol, who she got to call Gran now, was the next to arrive.

Sam helped her settle in a chair before placing the baby in her arms. "Oh, she's so beautiful. I knew all along the two of you would make the best babies together."

Sam groaned. "Gran…"

She winked up at him. "You give credit where credit is due, boy. My matchmaking skills, along with God's help, brought the two of you together."

Fiona giggled but Sam shook his head at her. "Don't you think we had something to do with it?"

Gran snorted. "Not at all. If either of you had your way, you'd still be stubborn and single right now. You needed someone to push you out of the muck you were stuck in."

Sam continued a good-natured argument with his grandmother, but Fiona couldn't help enjoying the exchange. She was fully accepted into this family now, so she got a front-row seat to their happiness at spending time together. And better yet, she got to share a piece of that happiness.

Gran finally gave up the baby to Sam and came over and gave Fiona a kiss on the cheek. "I told you that my grandson would be a good match for you and that you needed someone in your life. Aren't you glad you listened to me?"

Fiona laughed. "Yes, I am. I couldn't be happier."

Gran gave her a satisfied smile. "Your nana would be proud of you. I'm happy I can share a granddaughter with my friend now. I promised her I would take care of you, too."

Fiona felt a wave of love for the woman who was her nana's best friend. They were both so special to her, and now her daughter had two such strong women in her heritage.

Gran winked at Fiona. "And I think that your slow cooker recipes are improving."

Fiona groaned. She had tried for years now to improve on her cooking. While she had made baby steps, she hadn't yet mastered much skill. Gran and Sam faithfully tried everything that she put in front of them. Maybe one of these days she would get it right.

Gran liked to tease her that she messed things up on purpose just so that she had an excuse to keep visiting her every day, but Fiona really seemed to get mixed up when it came to spices and cooking times. She just had too many things on her mind. Sam just kissed her when she was frustrated and said that she was perfect in every other way, but he loved that she kept trying.

After Gran left the room, the baby started to fuss and Sam rushed into action. Fiona hid her smile as he cradled their baby in his arms and rocked her like a pro. The nurse and nurses' aide watched from the doorway, their eyes wide.

"I haven't seen too many fathers be able to pick it up like you can," the nurse said.

Her assistant nodded. "Yeah, most parents can't do it right away. This is amazing, especially for your first child."

Sam beamed at Fiona, his eyes only on his family, not the women heaping him with praise. "I had the best teacher."

Her heart fluttered at his words, but Sam's face tightened as the healthcare workers kept babbling with excitement about what a good father he was as they did their checks on Fiona and the baby.

"What's wrong?" she asked when they finally left.

Sam picked their daughter up out of the bassinet and bounced her gently in his arms, pacing around the room. "I don't understand why men get the praise for doing the bare minimum like picking up a baby when she cries while you did all the work to bring this baby into the world."

Fiona bit back her smile. "Well, you are really good at caring for babies. And I'm sure I will be appreciative when you let me sleep sometimes when she cries during the night."

He shook his head. "Still, it doesn't seem fair."

Fiona didn't mind that Sam got some attention because he was going to be an amazing father. He had been an amazing uncle to Hannah and Hazel and had so far been a wonderful husband to her. All their fears about not being able to have a happy marriage were unfounded.

Fiona let out a contented sigh as she listened to Sam humming out soothing words to their daughter, who was starting to fuss. There was no better sound in the entire world than her two favorite people being happy together. Everything she needed was in this room. Fiona leaned back against the pillow, her eyes starting to droop. She didn't want to fall asleep. No dream would be better that this reality.

Sam laid his sleeping daughter next to his dozing wife and pulled the chair next to the bed even closer.

To think that he hadn't wanted a family at one point in his life. His heart was so full of love for the two people in this room, he couldn't imagine being without them.

His job did not get any easier, but he pushed himself harder every day, knowing that the people in danger were loved by someone out in the world just as much as he loved Fiona and their baby. If he ever found himself in a situation that was difficult to get out of, his girls provided him with the motivation to keep going.

His epiphany had been correct—having someone to come home to made him more determined. He didn't avoid dangerous situations like he feared he would, but he had a reason to get out of them now. And that made him a better firefighter.

Sam let his wife and baby sleep while he went to grab a cup of coffee and visit his family in the waiting room. He was surprised that they were still there.

"You should take the girls home and put them in bed," Sam told Benjamin, who had a sleeping child curled into either side of him.

His brother's lips turned up. "Hazel wouldn't have it. She put her hands on her hips and gave me such a scowl and said she wasn't leaving until she met her cousin."

Sam covered his mouth to keep the laugh from bursting out and waking his nieces. "Sounds like her. I'm sure the baby will wake up hungry in a bit and once she has eaten, they will be up for visitors again. Really, though, you could come back tomorrow."

Benjamin shook his head. "You all spent so much time waiting around this hospital for me, I might as well get a feeling for what it's like on the other side of the situation."

Benjamin had healed well from his injuries. Only some scarring on his face and a slight limp were the reminders of the accident from two years ago.

"There was much more worrying going on back then, but the cafeteria food is still the same bland fare, if you want the real experience," Sam teased.

"Hazel has already demanded some of their chicken nuggets, so they must not be too bad."

Sam plopped down in the chair across from his brother. "I'm exhausted. How did you guys go through this twice?"

Benjamin gave him a sad smile. "Beth was a warrior when she delivered, just like your wife. The second time was a bit easier. I was more helpful rather than panicked."

Sam only hoped that was true. He leaned over and tucked Hannah's long blond curl behind her ear in her sleep. She had grown into a sweet toddler, following her hero Hazel into all kinds of mischief.

"I do have one leg up over you, though."

Benjamin arched an eyebrow. "Oh, yeah?"

Sam pointed between the two girls. "I've had practice handling babies. I'm a bottle-feeding pro. And my skills with loading a car seat are unmatched."

Benjamin chuckled. "You do have a bit more experience than the average first-time dad, but I have a feeling the baby will still surprise you. When you crash and burn, give me a call."

Sam rolled his eyes at his big brother's confidence in his downfall. He bit back a smile, though. It had taken a while and about a year of therapy for Ben to return to his old self. There would always be sadness and grief over the loss of Bethany, but he had gotten to a place where he was able to live without her and raise their daughters. He had even started talking about dating again sometime soon, but was nervous to get out there in the world.

"You will when the time is right," their mother had told him. And of course, Gran had several ladies in mind who would be perfect for him.

"Oh, by the way, speaking of you and my girls, Hazel is thrilled about her new cousin but is a little worried, too," Benjamin said.

Sam's brows furrowed. "What? Why?"

Ben rubbed his daughter's back in her sleep. "The two of you have been close since then and she's concerned you won't have time for her now that the baby is here."

Hannah fidgeted next to her dad and blinked up at Sam with big eyes. "Me, too, Unkie."

She had taken to calling him that once she started talking, and Hazel had never stopped, despite being in kindergarten and knowing the word *uncle*.

He held out his arms. "Come here, Hannahbear."

She scooched off the chair next to her dad and leaped into Sam's arms. He felt a tug on his sleeve and turned to see Hazel standing there. "You, too, Hazelnut. Bring it in."

She hugged his other side. "I want both of you to know that you will always be my special girls. I only took care of you for a short amount of time, but I will always be your uncle who loves you so much. I would be sad if I got to spend less time with you."

Hazel blinked up at him, not believing his words. "But you will be too busy being a daddy now."

Sam sighed and pulled her closer. "It's true that the

new baby will keep us busy for a while, but you can come out and help whenever you want."

Hazel perked up at that. "I can take care of the baby?"

Sam tilted his head. "Of course, as the bigger cousin, that's your job."

Hazel considered his words. "I learned how to read a book in school. I will read her bedtime stories like you and Fi did for me."

Sam told her that it sounded perfect, and she went on with a list of things she could do for her new cousin. Benjamin covered his mouth from across from them to hide his laugh. Hazel would probably insist on coming over as much as possible and probably would be more of a hindrance than a help. But he also had a feeling that they wouldn't mind either way.

Hannah elbowed him. "I help, too?"

He kissed the top of her head. "Of course, Hannah-bear. Your new cousin is going to need to know which toys are best once she's able to hold them."

Hannah's eyes got wide. "I tell her all the good ones."

He left a few minutes later to check on his wife and daughter. They were still asleep, but he sat by their side for a while, content in watching them. He must have dozed off, because a squeeze of his hand woke him up.

"Hey, I'm glad you finally crashed. You were running on adrenaline for a while," Fiona said.

He shrugged. "I'm not the one who brought her into the world. You're the one that needs the most rest."

Fiona gave him a happy smile as he looked down at their baby. "We really need to settle on a name. Your grandmother is insisting on using her name."

Sam tapped his chin. "I was thinking about that."

"Carol?"

He shook his head. "No... I mean yes...kind of. I think we should name her after both our grandmothers, since they kind of brought us together."

Fiona looked at him thoughtfully. "Elizabeth Carol?"

He smiled. "Sounds perfect."

The baby squirmed in Fiona's arms and Sam scooped her up, happy for a chance to hold her again. An hour was too long. "It's all right, little Lizzie. Daddy's here now."

Fiona told the nurse it was all right to allow Benjamin and the girls back and they burst into the room with excitement.

The two older cousins were fascinated by Lizzie and promised all the things they were going to do with her. Fiona watched in surprise. "They have it all planned out."

Sam grinned at his wife. "I maybe told them that we would need their help."

Fiona didn't object, accepting hugs from the little girls when their attention shifted to their aunt. "We help every day, Fi," Hazel promised.

Fiona squeezed the girl to her chest gently. With their nieces next to them, Sam was reminded of the time they were a temporary family unit.

Though he had to return the girls home to their father, the time with them had forever changed his life. Learning to care for Hannah and Hazel had taught him to open his heart to a family of his own.

Not only were the girls still in his life, but he had a wife and a daughter now. At first, he thought that his nieces would displace his life for a short while, but they had paved the way for his forever family.

Sam leaned over and kissed all four girls on the head.

Hazel looked up at him with a disgruntled look on her face. "Unkie, you gotta fix this baby. She stinks."

They all laughed as Sam pulled his daughter into his arms and carried her over to the changing table. Benjamin crossed to him and took over.

"I owe you about a thousand baby-care favors, and Fiona about the same number," he said.

Sam didn't need to be told twice. He climbed into bed next to Fiona. He let out an *oof* as Hazel plopped down to sit on his legs and Hannah climbed up in his lap. After Ben laid his niece down in the bassinet and went to get more coffee, Fiona, Sam and the girls all cuddled together to watch the baby sleep.

* * * * *

If you liked this story from Julie Brookman,
check out her previous Love Inspired book,

Their Business Betrothal

Available now from Love Inspired!
Find more great reads at www.LoveInspired.com.

Dear Reader:

I hope you enjoyed reading this story! When my husband and I were in training to become foster parents, we noticed that many of the other families in the room were kinship placement families. This means that they were grandparents, aunts, siblings, etc. that stepped up to the plate when kids in their family needed a stable home, even if only for a short while. The open hearts and kindness of these people just awed me, and I've been wanting to write a story to reflect their sacrifice. Sam's story was born out of this.

Before we adopted our kids, we encountered a plethora of dedicated social workers who went above and beyond to support the welfare of children. They gave their all every day and had to be with families at their worst. It takes an incredibly big heart and strong will to do their job every day. Fiona was inspired by all these incredible people, who more than deserve their own happily ever afters.

I plan to explore more stories about people like Sam and Fiona in my future books. I'm working on a new story that I hope you'll love.

One of my favorite things is to connect with my readers! You can visit me at my website at www.authorjuliebrookman.com. There, you can sign up for my monthly newsletter, find out how to follow me on social media, or send me a message.

Thanks for reading!
Julie Brookman

COMING NEXT MONTH FROM
Love Inspired

THEIR AMISH SECRET
Amish Country Matches • by Patricia Johns

Putting the past behind her is all single Amish mother Claire Glick wants. But when old love Joel Beiler shows up on her doorstep in the middle of a harrowing storm, it could jeopardize everything she's worked for—including her best-kept secret...

THE QUILTER'S SCANDALOUS PAST
by Patrice Lewis

Esther Yoder's family must sell their mercantile store, and when an out-of-town buyer expresses interest, Esther is thrilled. Then she learns the buyer is Joseph Kemp—the man responsible for ruining her reputation. Can she set aside her feelings for the sake of the deal?

THE RANCHER'S SANCTUARY
K-9 Companions • by Linda Goodnight

With zero ranching experience, greenhorn Nathan Garrison has six months to reopen an abandoned guest ranch—or lose it forever. So he hires scarred cowgirl Monroe Matheson to show him the ropes. As they work together, will secrets from the past ruin their chance at love?

THE BABY INHERITANCE
Lazy M Ranch • by Tina Radcliffe

Life changes forever when rancher Drew Morgan inherits his best friend's baby. But when he learns professor Sadie Ross is also part of the deal, things get complicated. Neither one of them is ready for domestic bliss, but sweet baby Mae might change their minds...

MOTHER FOR A MONTH
by Zoey Marie Jackson

Career-weary Sienna King yearns to become a mother, and opportunity knocks when know-it-all reporter Joel Armstrong comes to her with an unusual proposal. Putting aside their differences, they must work together to care for his infant nephew, but what happens when their pretend family starts to feel real?

THE NANNY NEXT DOOR
Second Chance Blessings • by Jenna Mindel

Grieving widower Jackson Taylor moves to small-town Michigan for the sake of his girls. When he hires his attractive next-door neighbor, Maddie Williams, to be their nanny, it could be more than he bargained for as the line between personal and professional starts to blur...

LICNM0323

HARLEQUIN
PLUS

Try the best multimedia subscription service for romance readers like you!

Read, Watch and Play.

Experience the easiest way to get the romance content you crave.

Start your **FREE TRIAL** at
<u>www.harlequinplus.com/freetrial</u>.